After

the

Before

Times

The Shadows of Innocence

DIANE STRINGAM TOLLEY

1

Summary: In Post-Apocalyptic Canada, a young worker struggles to understand her world and her feelings in the face of slavery and programmed thinking.

ISBN-9798340074218

Cover design © 2024 by Diane Stringam Tolley

DEDICATION

To all the Families
Yours
is the Important Work

In the Before Times, Jack was a pilot. After the Before Times, he was my hero.

PART ONE

CHAPTER ONE

I looked up.

Boots. White boots.

Slowly, I allowed my eyes to move upwards. Long, flowing, white robes. A bend that could possibly be knees. Hands braced on the heavily carved arms of the chair. More robes. And finally, a chin.

My eyes stopped of their own volition.

Never before had I dared to look a Master in the face.

He made a noise. A…throat-clearing sort of noise.

I took a deep breath of sun-baked earth and clean, washed bodies and forced my eyes higher.

Lips. Nose. Finally, eyes.

There I again stopped. The eyes were the colour of the earth, after it had been tilled. A dark, rich brown.

And they were looking at me. Studying me.

I dropped my gaze once more to the ground and felt warmth steal up from my neck and into my face.

"Red."

The voice came from in front and above me. I felt my brows draw down in confusion.

"Red."

This time, I understood the word. Someone was speaking to *me*.

Startled, I glanced up unwillingly.

It was the Master. And he had risen to his feet and was holding out one hand towards me.

For several moments, I stared at it, uncomprehendingly. Never, since my beginning, had a Master noticed, or even acknowledged me.

The sight was truly frightening.

"Take his hand, Red," a voice behind me whispered. "Get to your feet."

I jumped and almost squeaked in alarm. Teacher, from the Growing buildings, had obviously seen my hesitation and had come, one last time, to instruct me through a difficulty.

"Take his hand," she repeated.

I felt my mouth drop open in horror. Touch him? A Master?

"Red, take his hand."

I took a deep breath and slowly reached out. My breath stopping in my throat as my blindly searching fingers encountered . . . warmth. I nearly snatched my hand away, but the Master was too fast for me. As soon as we connected, he tightened his fingers around mine and pulled.

I came to my feet shakily, and for the first, and only, time, was face to face with a Master.

I dropped my gaze to proper position, allowing myself to see only his mouth, and I watched as his lips moved and he pronounced the words that I had been awaiting since my beginning 16 years before.

"This young-one has fulfilled the learning and growing stages of her life," he said. "Therefore, I pronounce her grown and ready to accept the responsibility as a full worker in our colony. In keeping with the traditions of this moment, and having studied the records of her raising, I also give her a name that suits her and that will attend her for the rest of her days. I call her Listener."

After 16 seasons of being known by a physical feature or skill, as were all of us in the Growing buildings, I finally had my adult name.

I was very careful not to let my discomfort show.

Of all of the talents that I had exhibited during my growing years, the most notable being an affinity for numbers, the Master had been made aware of, and chosen, my most unfortunate. My love of listening to other people converse.

I now knew that my weakness would mark me for life.

The group gathered together was silent, as they always were. I could not tell what they were thinking or whether they thought it a particularly unusual name. They merely mouthed it a few times to commit it to memory, then reached out their hands and touched my shoulder gently, using the first and second fingers in the traditional salute. It was the only time that we would be allowed to make deliberate contact, and they immediately drew back and returned to their various duties.

I was permitted to return to the Growing Buildings one last time to collect my few items of acquired necessities. I took my leave of the nine other young-ones and was escorted to the Stable to receive the room assignment that would be mine for what I understood would be the rest of my life. But in reality was only for the rest of my life on Master's farm.

A much shorter term.

CHAPTER TWO

My first days as an adult were difficult. I did not feel any different than I had only a short time before when I had been considered a young-one. There had been no dramatic change that had made me suddenly wise and mature. To me the mere passing of another anniversary of my Beginning was just that—the passing of another day.

But to everyone else in the colony, I was suddenly an adult, capable of carrying my portion of the work and responsibility. Able to make decisions necessary to the job I was given, and totally in control of myself in any situation which confronted me.

To attempt to describe the confusion and outright fear of those days is beyond my capability. Maybe it is enough to say that I was confused and frightened. And completely alone.

A worker led me to a room on the East End of the Stable and left me standing in the corridor. I leaned forward, peering hesitantly through the doorway into a tiny area lighted by a single candle in a sconce by the door.

There was only room for a sleeping mat, a small cupboard, barely higher than my waist, and a tiny table against the wall just inside the door. The mat, I was used to. We had slept on similar ones in the Growing buildings. But the cupboard was new to me, though I knew what it was for. And more strange still was the equipment that stood silently on it.

As a young one, always I had been washed and groomed in a small building adjoining the main structure where we lived. We had huge tubs in which to wash our hands and faces, and even larger containers for bathing.

Here, atop my little cupboard, was a small blue china bowl, hardly bigger than a large soup plate, and a matching china pitcher filled with water. A cake of soap sat in a tiny dish to one side, and a length of towelling hung from a loop of heavy wire at the side. It was obvious to me that I was expected to wash here. I had no idea how I was going to be able to clean all of me in that tiny container. Worse still was the thought of how warm and comfortable my baths had been and how I was going to miss them.

I heaved a sigh. Being an adult may have seemed an adventure when one looked forward to it as a young-one, but being an adult was much different when one actually became one.

In the bottom of my cupboard were two doors, which opened outward from the centre of the unit. I reached for the tiny knobs and pulled. Inside, I was surprised to find a stack of neatly folded material, in the same blue colour as the robe that I had always worn.

I reached for the folds on top and realised that I held a uniform, which had trousers and shirt in one piece. I had seen the other adult workers wear such a garment, but it never occurred to me that I would be expected to do so also.

Beside the stack of uniforms, I found another pile, undergarments, also clean and folded. I was reaching for them when a knock on my door startled me. The door swung open and I caught my first glimpse of Meg.

She was small, not much taller than I, and slender, with black hair cut in the style worn by all of the workers. I could not look her in the face for some time, but finally found the courage to do so and was surprised by the calm expression in her very dark eyes.

"Listen, I welcome you to the Stable," she said, setting a tray she held down on the table and giving me the now-familiar salute. "I am Meg. I have the care of these rooms. I am here to explain a few things to you."

I stood quietly and waited for her to continue.

"I see that you have found your uniforms and undergarments," she went on. "Good. You must wear these at all times. Your boots have been ordered and should be here soon. Until they arrive, you are allowed to wear your slippers."

I glanced down and wiggled my toes. We young-ones had always worn a sort of heavy cloth shoe, cut of thick pieces of felt. They were warm and comfortable, but seemed to wear out with amazing quickness.

"You will do your morning and evening wash here, in this small basin," Meg continued, indicating the china that I had already noted. "Twice a week, you will be allowed to go to the Toilet buildings in the courtyard to bathe."

I heaved a sigh of relief at her words, casting a quick look at the basin and pitcher.

Meg looked at me, but made no comment. "After you bathe, you will place all soiled garments in the baskets provided and collect replacements from the clean stacks there. Supplies for moon-days are also available there—I will show you later. Your morning and evening meals will be taken here. But after today, your midday meal will be eaten while you are working. Do you have any questions?"

I merely shook my head, too insecure and unsure to attempt any speech.

Meg nodded. "Perhaps you will think of something as your day continues," she said. "I will leave you alone to change and eat." She indicated the tray. "Young Master will be here in a few minutes to escort you to your new duties, so please be quick."

She turned and left me alone with my new uniform clutched to my chest. The soft closing of the door startled me into activity, and I pulled off my robe and undergarments and donned the new, wiggling uncomfortably at the unusual feeling of the cloth around my legs. I balled my old clothing together and set it in a small basket by the door.

Then I sat, cross-legged, on my mat to make a quick meal and to await Young Master.

I did not wait long. In a few moments, Meg again tapped on my door and swung it open. I rose to my feet and she nodded when she saw that I was ready. She bent over and picked up my small bundle of clothing and led me down the dark corridor to the outside door.

There in the sunshine, I saw Young Master for the first time.

He was tall, as was Master, but with very dark hair, and was dressed in the familiar manner of the masters—in white. He looked at me and just for a moment, I chanced to catch his eyes. I

10

gasped at my own temerity and immediately lowered my gaze, but not before I had noticed the deep brown colour of his eyes and the slight frown that marred the smooth skin between them.

He turned abruptly, without speaking, and I followed him across the compound to the far eastern side. There I saw a building, rectangular in shape with windows all around the upper section of the north half. A door was set among all those windows, and it, too, had a window in the upper section. The result was a room that was amazingly bright. I blinked a couple of times as we stepped inside. It was as light as if we still stood in the courtyard.

Young Master strode over to a huge desk, which stood in a corner. It was bare, except for a large book lying to one side. He reached for the book and indicated that I should come over and take a seat in the chair beside the desk.

I did so, carefully keeping my eyes on the book that he opened for me.

I saw familiar columns of numbers. As my practised eye went down the long lists, I could see that here was recorded all the business that went on at Master's farm and another place called the 'Museum'. Entries for expenditures as well as income were duly recorded.

I nodded my head. Here was something I understood.

Young Master indicated the stack of receipts and other papers that were stuffed in the front of the book and explained a little of the business end of Master's operation, his voice flat and impersonal.

I did not have any difficulty understanding what he told me. This was what I had trained so long for, and I was anxious to start work. I was equally anxious for him to leave. For some reason, his presence made me feel…odd.

Several times, I caught myself stealing glances at him; at his hands as he leaned near and rested them on the desk; at his feet as they made the floor creak beside my chair. It was almost as though my eyes, of their own accord, were trying to take in all the details at once.

11

Finally, I was both relieved and disappointed when he turned and walked to the door. Just inside the doorway, he stopped. I looked up inquiringly, but he simply stood there, staring at me. I was just working up the courage to try to look into his face when he turned abruptly and walked down the stairs, closing the door firmly behind him.

I shook off the strange feelings that remained after his departure and set to work. In what seemed a very short time, but was in reality several hours, Young Master was back, ready to escort me to the Stable.

Thus he laid a pattern which was to become daily routine for the next four years of my life.

CHAPTER THREE

In that first year, I got to know every facet of Master's business and knew that he prospered. My days slid one into another, each much the same as the others. My duties never changed and very little that was different ever seemed to happen.

Except for two incidents.

As the days lengthened into summer, the extended hours of sunlight made it uncomfortably warm in my little office. Young Master got into the habit of opening all the windows before he left each morning and closing them when he came to collect me at the end of every day. All that summer, along with the cooling breezes, the sounds from outside also drifted in.

I was at work trying to balance a long column of figures that scoffed at my efforts, when I heard loud voices.

Just outside.

I knew that the gardening crew was labouring out there among Master's vegetables on the East Side of the office, but had paid them little mind, engrossed in my work.

I raised my head and craned my neck in an effort to see what was going on without being seen myself. At first, I could not make out the words, but the loud voices continued, one of them rising steadily in pitch until it was nearly a scream. I finally could not control my curiosity any longer and half rose to peer over the windowsill.

"You idiots!" A small female worker, dressed in soil-stained blue uniform, broad straw hat shading her face, was standing in the middle of the garden, trowel in hand.

Several other workers had paused in their labours and were staring at her.

"Keep working!" someone shouted.

They ducked their heads and complied.

I turned slightly, and caught my breath as I recognized Master, standing to one side of the garden. He turned his head towards me and my heart gave an uncomfortable leap until I realized that he was looking, not at me as I had first supposed, but below me, at someone standing near the building wall under my window.

"Take her," he said to the unseen persons, indicating the female worker with a jerk of his head.

Two male workers moved into my sight and started towards the female.

She pointed the trowel at them defiantly. "Can't any of you see what is going on here?" she demanded loudly. "Don't you realize that they are no different from the rest of us? That we are all the same?"

"Take her!" Master's voice was suddenly louder.

"We have rights!" Her voice had risen, once more, to a scream.

Two male workers grabbed her arms and were attempting to pull her out of the garden. The Master stood to one side, both hands on his hips. "Get her out of here!"

The female was resisting violently and began screeching incoherently at everyone. As she struggled, I saw her wide-brimmed hat slip to one side and finally tumble to the ground.

I gasped as I saw the colour of her hair. It was the same unusual colour as mine, a flaming red-gold, though hers was lightly streaked with a lighter colour—perhaps grey? Never before had I seen a head like mine, and I almost felt as if it were me out there defying everyone. For just a moment, I could feel my heart pumping and my chest swell as an unusual and unknown emotion swept over me.

The female looked at the other workers, all with heads bowed and continuing their work.

Then, she went limp in the grasp of the two workers and with equal suddenness, the emotion that had filled me was gone, leaving me feeling weak and tired. I heard Master tell the two male workers to escort the female to her room and return to their duties. They left, leading her between them. She walked slowly, dragging her feet, never once lifting her head.

Master watched them go, then suddenly turned and looked right toward me. I quickly ducked out of sight, and had no idea

14

whether or not he saw me, but his action had frightened me and I busied myself with my familiar ledgers once more.

I never saw that worker again. A few days later, a receipt crossed my desk, and I duly noted that one female worker, aged 36 years, had been sold to a farmer that I had never heard of before. Just for a moment, I thought of the worker standing in the garden, defying everyone, and that same strange wave of emotion swept over me. I could not put a name to it, but it lingered and made my work difficult.

In fact, for many, many days, I could see that small figure in my mind, defying everyone. Each time the memory swept over me, I would again be overtaken by those strange emotions. Finally, as the months passed, the memory plagued me less and less, until, finally, it was forgotten in the sameness of my daily life.

The second incident, however, was even more disturbing as it involved me directly and was confusing, unnerving and painful.

My day had begun much as any other. It was late winter and the sky was heavy with cloud and continually threatening snow. Young Master had been in to start the fire in the small stove near my desk and the chill was just off the room. I had removed my heavy outer clothing and mittens, finally able to begin the work that I had laid out while waiting for the ink to thaw.

I was deeply involved in a complicated series of numbers when the door banged open and one of the male workers, Rodney, came in. I had never spoken to him, but had seen him many times and knew his name. It was so unusual for anyone to come into the office during the day that I simply gaped at him, speechless. The fact that it was another worker who had come in finally registered and I leaped to my feet, expecting that some emergency had arisen.

"What is it, Rodney?" I asked, reaching for the coat draped over the back of my chair. He didn't answer, but pushed the door shut and moved close to me, grabbing for my coat. I was surprised by his move and allowed him to take it out of unresisting hands.

For several seconds he stood there, just holding it and it was then I noticed that he was shaking and that he held my coat so tightly his knuckles showed white. He finally threw it down on the floor and came once more towards me.

His eyes gleamed strangely and I backed slowly before him, still not understanding, but now thoroughly frightened. He looked odd and…not quite sane. Soon, backed up against my desk, I was forced to stop. Carefully, I slid along it and finally felt the cold of the window against my back. I was trapped in the corner between the two. As he came closer, my mind seemed to fly in circles. In my panic, I couldn't decide what to do. I tried to dodge past him and he lunged at me, knocking me back against the window.

The cold glass shattered and bit deeply into my shoulder blade. I cried out and instinctively lunged forward, away from it, but Rodney was there, and suddenly his hands were tearing at my uniform. He pulled at it futilely for a brief moment, then locked both hands into the neck and split it to the waist, buttons popping and flying everywhere.

He pushed me back onto the desk and my books and papers slid off into a heap on the floor. I doubled up my knees and tried to use my feet to push him away, but he was tearing at my uniform again, and I gasped as I felt the sturdy fabric part. He pulled it off one shoulder and I cried out as it rubbed across the torn skin. Then I tried to push his hands away as he began tearing at my undershirt. Again, he grabbed the neck and the soft garment came away in one pull. For a moment, he stared at it, touching a finger to the bloodstains which now covered it. As his attention moved momentarily from me, I tried to leap past him. He was too quick for me, however, and once more forced me back against the desk, dropping the torn shirt as he rolled me onto my back and began wrenching at my uniform again.

My chest was completely exposed by this time and I screamed as his hands contacted bare skin. No one had ever touched me before and my body rebelled. I jerked up against him, almost causing him to lose his balance, but he easily recovered and threw his weight down on me, knocking my breath away.

16

I could smell him as he panted in my face and I felt nauseous, but with his greater weight pinning me down, I could hardly breathe and I stared helplessly into his eyes. He shifted his weight a little, allowing me to take a breath, but a surge of hope quickly died as I felt his hands moving again and I groaned as I felt the fabric across my back and hips begin to give way. Then he was gone, as if some great wind had plucked him off me and thrown him across the room.

I slid quickly off the desk, grateful for the respite, and crouched into the corner between the desk and the broken window. I waited for him to renew his attack and was frantically looking for something, anything to help me when I realised that we were no longer alone.

Young Master stood between us, breathing heavily and watching as Rodney struggled to regain his feet. As soon as the smaller man was standing, Young Master folded up his fingers and hit him in the face, knocking him over again. This time Rodney stayed down, sanity slowly returning to his eyes, followed quickly by fear.

"Get up and return to your room," Young Master said, his voice deadly calm. "Wait there for me."

Rodney struggled once more to his feet and staggered towards the door. He paused in the opening, balancing himself with a hand on the sill and turned to look at me.

"Liss, I…" he began but Young Master cut him off.

"Say nothing!" he said, still in that quiet, deadly voice. "Out!" Rodney ducked his head and left. I watched him as he stumbled across the yard towards the Stable.

I rose slowly and turned to Young Master.

He was looking at me, and his eyes suddenly flared in an expression that reminded me of Rodney's only a few moments before. I clutched the edges of my uniform together and backed away from him.

"Liss," he said softly, using the workers' name for me. "Liss, let me help you." He was walking towards me and I felt the return of panic. I crouched back down on the floor and scrambled into

17

the space under my desk, placing my back to the farthest wall and preparing to kick at him when he drew near.

He knelt down just out of reach and looked at me for a moment. "Liss," he said quietly. "Come out, I want to help you."

But I couldn't trust him. I had seen the same thing in his eyes that I had seen in Rodney's. I didn't understand it and it terrified me. He sat there without speaking for a short while longer, then he rose to his feet and moved away.

"Listen," he said, and I relaxed slightly as I recognised his usual impersonal voice. "Come out now so I can help you." I leaned out of my shelter and looked up at him. He wasn't looking at me, and had turned his back. Slowly, I moved into the room, ready to run, but he stayed where he was, turning his head only when I finally approached him.

"You probably haven't realised it," he said, "but you are bleeding quite badly and need attention. Let me look at your back." Obediently, I turned my back toward him and loosened the sides of my uniform so he could pull the fabric down and look at my shoulder. He sucked in his breath and gently touched the sticky skin. Then he reached past me and grabbed the torn, bloody shirt from off the desk. "Is this yours?" he asked, unnecessarily.

I nodded and bent my head, trying to understand the quivering, aching lump that seemed to have formed in my chest. I felt his gentle touch once again as he dabbed at my back with the shirt. Then he spread it out over the wound.

"Pull your uniform back up, if you can," he said, holding his makeshift bandage in place.

I did so, gasping at the pain that shot through my back as I flexed the muscles.

"Now I'll take you to the hospital," he said, looking about and finally spotting my coat on the floor. He picked it up and shook it, laying it across my shoulders. He started to push me towards the door, but my legs were weak and refused to obey me.

Then the room suddenly started spinning. I tried to place a shaking hand upon the nearest flat surface, not realising that it was the stove.

Young Master cried out and grabbed for me, but not before the palm of my hand had made contact with the scorching metal.

I felt no pain, but instinctively gasped and tried to push the burned portion into my mouth.

Then Young Master had my hand between his.

I looked at him from what seemed a great distance. The room was growing darker and I looked around in surprise. Then I was lying on the floor, wondering briefly how I had gotten there.

Young Master looked down at me for an instant, as surprised as I was. Then he scooped me up in his arms and carried me outside.

I started shivering violently as the cold air hit me, and he broke into run across the compound. Numbly, I let my head fall back against his chest—oddly calmed by the feel of firm muscles beneath my cheek.

Halfway to the hospital, he suddenly stopped. I tried to turn my head to see what was happening, but my vision blurred abruptly and I weakly leaned my head once more against his chest.

Young Master spoke briefly to someone. "I have to get her to the hospital, Father," he said. "I'll tell you everything later!"

Then he resumed his run towards the hospital.

I did not understand the conversation and I had never heard of anyone called 'Father'. But thinking made my head swim. I closed my eyes.

The healer met us at the door and directed Young Master to take me into one of the inner rooms. We went down a long hall, still at a run and his feet slipped a little as he spun into a doorway. Gently, he set me on a long table covered in a clean white cloth, then grabbed the Healer's arm and whispered a few words into his ear. The healer nodded and Young Master came over to me.

"Healer will look after you now, Liss," he said quietly. "I have some things to attend to."

I just stared at him stupidly, shivering.

He stood there for a moment more, looking at me strangely, then he was gone.

The healer came to me and began to remove my coat. As he pulled the sleeve off my shoulder, a sudden pain shot up my arm and made me catch my breath.

"It will be over in a moment," he said. "I just have to have a look at your shoulder, Liss. Then we can see about your hand." He eased the sleeve off my shoulder and peeled my uniform deftly to my waist, handing me a clean cloth to cover myself. He grunted to himself as he worked and I glimpsed another healer come into the room with a tray containing a bowl of liquid and some instruments.

They gave me something salty to drink, and then I was pressed down onto my stomach and told to lie still. I began to feel very warm and relaxed and seemed to be floating somewhere just above the table.

Finally, I lost consciousness altogether and woke some time later, feeling a little stiff, but warmly blanketed and comfortable. I tried to sit up and cried out as my muscles protested. I felt over my shoulder with my good hand and realised that I had been neatly bandaged.

My cry had brought someone out of the shadowy hall. She glided up to the mat and knelt down, reaching for my hand. She placed fingers on my wrist and stared into space for a time, then she patted my head and left.

The Healer came in shortly after.

"You have a nasty wound on your shoulder and down your back," he said. "Even without the damage to the muscle, it would have been a tricky wound to close. We have stitched you up, but those muscles will take a while to heal." He went on. "The burn on your hand is superficial and will heal quite quickly, barring infection. I have told the Master that you are to be given light work only for many days. He agrees with me. I'm glad your usual duties are not heavily physical."

He hesitated beside my bed, looking like he wanted to say something more.

"Was there something else?" I asked, my voice sounding faint and weak.

"It is this worker that broke into the office," he said. "Have you ever spoken to him, or has he ever…touched you before?"

I could feel my eyes getting big. Speaking between workers was strictly monitored and completely limited to work. Touching was unheard of! If I had said or done anything with that Worker, would I be punished, or worse…sold? My mind seemed to freeze at the thought.

He realised that I was afraid. "I am not accusing you," he said gently. "Young Master is wondering if you have ever encouraged this Worker in any way."

"Encouraged?" I was lost. "I do not even remember ever speaking to him," I said, closing my eyes as I tried to think. "I barely remembered his name."

"I thought not," he said, squeezing my hand. "That makes punishment much easier."

"Punishment!" I gasped. "Oh please, tell Young Master I have never talked to the Worker! I have never…! I did not ask him into the office…!"

"No, no, Miss," he soothed. "Not *your* punishment…his."

"Oh," I said weakly, relief washing over me. I lay there for several seconds. Then, quietly, "What will they do to him?"

"Do not worry about that," he said. "That is up to the Masters to decide. Young Master really is upset over this. I think that Worker will never bother you again."

"What will they do to him?" I asked again, my voice a little fainter.

"Now you drink this and rest for a while," the healer pressed another glass into my hand. "You get yourself healed and then we will see what is to be done."

Obediently, I drained the glass and handed it back to him, relaxing once more on the mat. He left the room and I turned the events of the day over in my mind, wondering what it had all been about. Slowly I drifted off to sleep.

I did not see Rodney for a long time, but no sales receipt crossed my desk. Then one day I noticed him taking a heavy team out towards one of the fields to begin spring ploughing. That he had been demoted to the position of heaviest labour must have been his punishment and I felt a brief, nameless twinge for him. His face as I last saw it stayed with me for a very long time.

As did the baffling feelings of fear and confusion that the whole episode had given me. For many months, I was haunted by it, even waking from sleep, sure that Rodney's hands were reaching for me from out of the shadows of my dreams.

Finally, as no further threat became apparent, even the dreams began to fade and I was once more calm within the confines of my little world.

Two more years passed and I did change into an adult. Slowly my new experiences supplanted those I remembered as a young-one. More and more, I was feeling like the person I was expected to be, with an adult perspective of the world around me. I was certain that I knew as much about life and everyone about me as there was to know. Only in looking back over years and experiences do I realise that I was a young-one still.

That my life was only just about to begin.

PART TWO

CHAPTER FOUR

The small square of light had been slowly making its way across the plain blue cover on my sleeping mat for the past fifteen minutes and I knew that the time was fast approaching when I would hear Meg's gentle tapping on my door and my day would begin. This was the best time of the day, when the glorious red-gold rays of sunlight found my little window and shone through to march with silent precision across my tiny room. Part of me—that which had remained even after I gave up being a young-one—always wakened first and wanted to be out and running in the wet, sweet grass.

Thoughts of crawling through windows or sneaking out before the all-important knock were slowly crushed by the weighty return of my common sense, however, as my sensible *adult* self became conscious and turned me cold with thoughts of the repercussions that such an act would create. I busied myself with a careful study of my small cubicle.

I had lived in the Worker's quarters for nearly four years, now, and all my leisure time had been spent within the confines of this small space. We were not allowed much free time, so there was little of a diversionary nature here - only a couple of weighty books that had been given to me to read by the Teachers. I seemed to have an unquenchable thirst for knowledge and the Masters encouraged all of us to read and study from their library as often as we could find the time from our duties. I took advantage of it.

My eyes wandered over the walls.

Once a year, as part of my duties, I took my records to Master's quarters. I was always seated on a chair just outside the front door while Master took the books and did a preliminary check to ensure that everything was there, and, during that short

23

time, I had caught glimpses of walls hung with pictures of scenes and persons.

I was reminded briefly of little Artist, who had been in the Growing buildings with me, and her slender, talented fingers. She had been very tiny and sickly-looking, but had learned to paint the most amazing scenes on tightly stretched cloth. Materials that I would have used to cover the cracks in the walls became magic in Artist's little hands and scenes from all over Master's property had soon filled our whitewashed walls.

Often, I had thought how nice it would be to have a few of these beautiful pictures to gaze upon, but I made no attempt to adorn my bare walls. Only those things which had been present when I had been moved in or which were deemed absolutely necessary were there. In addition to my pallet on the floor, I still possessed two uniforms, a set of night-clothes, three sets of undergarments and one pair of heavy boots.

The rays of sunlight were pitilessly picking out the cracks and wear in the leather of those boots, brought about by nearly four years of constant use. Even to my inexperienced eyes, they were in need of being replaced. But now, my thoughts were of the fuss the making of those boots had created among the workers who were in charge of the manufacture and cleaning of our clothing.

The small size of my feet had forced the designing of a whole new pattern, and much time and effort was necessarily put into the task. I closed my eyes and remembered how I had been forced to wear my slippers for many days because of the delay in receiving by boots. The other workers had eyed me curiously. Different apparel was not a common sight.

Fortunately, the pattern would still be in existence, so a new pair of boots would not cause great problems for the workers.

My thoughts were interrupted by the awaited knock on my door. Meg poked her head in and gave me her usual morning greeting. "Daylight, Liss," she said softly. "Time to put another day on your list of accomplishments." She gathered up the soiled towel that I had thrown into the basket by the door and set a small pitcher of warm water beside my washbowl. Then she turned and

24

made her way back into the hallway. I could hear her soft tap on the next door and then I quickly rose to begin my day.

Meg was moving slowly about her duties. She was in her seventh month of Carrying and already, she was heavy and her mobility was becoming hampered. Her time of marking would soon arrive and I secretly hoped that her healing period would be brief and she would be able to go about her various duties with her usual light step once again.

I could not help but remember a young female worker that Master and Young Master had brought back from the fields in the back of the wagon. She lay unconscious on her back, and I could tell by her small protruding belly that she was Carrying. It was unusual for a worker to ride, and that sight alone would have aroused attention, but when they stopped the wagon before the hospital, carefully pulled the unconscious female out and carried her inside, many workers paused in their labours and openly watched. No one voiced any questions, however and I wondered if they were asking themselves the same things that I was.

I did not see the young woman come back out of the hospital, though I watched secretly for several days. A large wooden box was carried in at one point, but other than that I saw no signs of activity. Several days later, a note crossed my desk, reporting the death of the field hand Dori—age 21 and I concluded that this had been the Worker that we had all seen that day.

My mind wandered back to Meg as I finished washing and began to dress. It was 24 seasons since her own beginning, and Meg was considered old to be Carrying. She had not had an easy time taking—she had been sent up to the hospital 34 times before she 'caught'. It was with evident relief that she received the news that the process had been successful.

Master's female workers were each given four years, from the time they had 20 seasons until they gained 24. If in that time they failed to Carry, they were usually sent to another farm—perhaps one of those where proper care was not considered important.

25

With the knowledge that she was Carrying and that her marking was imminent, Meg was assured of her place here on Master's property. It was with relief that I heard the news, also. Meg had helped me during my time in the Stables, and I did not like to hear any suggestion that she may be taken away from us.

Meg had been in charge of the Stable for eight years now. It was she who saw to the cleaning and provisioning of our rooms. She also had charge of our meals, and saw that they were delivered to each of us to be eaten in solitude. She made me feel quiet and comfortable, just by being near, and the thought of her absence made me feel...well...empty inside.

Though most of my life was spent in solitude, somehow I still needed the presence of others. The one thing I missed most in my move from the Growing buildings was the chance to eat with the other young-ones around a large table in a huge room, though verbal converse between us was strictly forbidden. The feelings I had experienced during those times were a mystery to me, but they had been pleasurable and I felt their loss.

After washing and dressing, I tidied my mat and opened my door wide. Within seconds, Yetta, Meg's new helper came in with my meal. It was the usual fare, warm, fresh bread, a cup of chicory tea, dried fruit, and a slice of white cheese. It did not take me long to finish it. Within moments of clearing my tray, the bell sounded and the 20 of us were finally able to leave our rooms and gather in the courtyard outside to drink up the sunshine and to perform our bodily functions in the centrally located toilet building.

Stepping out of the small square building, I thought, as I always did that from a short distance away, we looked like several copies of the same person, wearing the same uniform and having our hair cut in an identical fashion.

Close up, however, the differences became more noticeable. We were none of us alike in height and weight, skin colour or facial features. My own skin was of an almost transparent white, and I was several inches shorter and several pounds lighter than any other. Another worker, Jimmy, was nearest to me in height and weight, though his skin was bordering on yellow, and Ross was a giant with skin the colour of the darkest of woods.

Ross was sitting on the tongue of a wagon, his head down. For a moment, I stared at him. Always, he seemed strange to me. No other worker on the farm looked quite like him, though Mia, a healer who had been in the Growing buildings with me, was almost as darkly coloured.

She was sitting on the ground a short distance from Ross and seemed to be gazing in his direction, as I was.

He raised his head suddenly and looked towards her and I was puzzled at the expression that came to both faces.

Odd.

It was then that another worker slowly exited our Stable and joined us. A…different worker. One I had never seen before.

His face seemed to have fallen inwards and its collapse had resulted in an intricate network of wrinkles that trailed right down his neck. Thick brows sprouted above his eyes, looking as though they needed…weeding. Sparse, white hair did not come close to covering his large, naked head.

I stared at that hair. Everyone, with the exception of me with my red-gold, had dark or completely black hair.

How unusual.

His eyes were a faded blue and sunken into his face so that the flesh hung about them, almost obscuring them from sight. But they were bright and I was startled to find them pinned on me.

I saw him look at my hair, then into my face. I lowered my eyes in confusion, but I could feel his gaze still on me.

I took a quick, nervous breath as he approached. Then another as he sat beside me in the dirt. I lowered my head still further.

Why a new worker would notice me, and then risk the wrath of the Masters by further seeking me out was beyond my comprehension.

I shrank away from him, trying to appear ignorant of his presence.

"Are you the worker named Liss?" the soft, deep voice came from beside me and could only have come from the new worker.

I nodded slightly, looking frantically around for some sign of a Master.

The worker sighed and, unthinkably, reached out and touched my hair.

I leaped to my feet, then froze as I realized that my action had attracted all eyes. As everyone's attention slowly turned elsewhere, I slid slowly along the wall of the Stable.

Away from him.

He got carefully to his feet and followed.

"I'm sorry, Liss," he said softly, glancing around. "I didn't mean to startle you. It's just that I've seen hair like yours before."

I stopped. "You mean that other worker?"

He frowned. "Other worker?"

"Yes. The one who was sold."

The air went out of him in a whoosh and he suddenly appeared even smaller.

"Sold?" he managed, finally. Weakly.

I stared at him. "Yes. At least a pair of seasons ago."

He leaned back against the wall. "It must be," he said softly.

I said nothing, but remained where I was.

He was looking at me again. "How old was this worker?"

"She was 36 when she was sold," I said. "The receipt came to me to enter into the books."

"Of course." He closed his eyes and I was surprised to see a trickle of water seep from beneath the lids.

For several seconds, he stood there, gently shaking his head and ignoring the moisture which was making tracks into the seams that lined his cheeks. I stared at them in fascination.

And that was when Young Master joined us.

After that, during our few stolen moments of relaxation in the morning sun, Jack, as I came to know him, would seek me out.

Through our stolen moments of conversation, I soon discovered that his shrunken features and wrinkled skin were a product of his great age. At more than ninety seasons, he had the

28

dubious distinction of being the oldest worker any of us had ever seen.

In point of fact, his lifetime stretched back into the Before Times. He spoke easily of provinces, countries, peoples, husbands, wives, love, automobiles, machines, and many other things so fantastic to my mind as to be unbelievable.

Once, when he was especially tired, he talked quietly of something truly horrifying.

He called it 'war'.

"It was the end of everything, Liss," he told me quietly, and as he spoke, his eyes began to stream water. Then he lapsed into silence.

I could not get him to mention this terrible thing again, and, indeed, hesitated to try; first, because of his obvious discomfort; and second, for the sake of safety.

For both of us.

Communication between any of us other than that required to facilitate our various duties was discouraged so strongly as to be forbidden. The exchange of experiences and ideas would most certainly result in punishment, or even sale. Thus they had to be kept brief.

And very, very secret.

We were, once more, standing side-by-side against the wall of the building, soaking up the first warm sunlight of the day.

"So, Liss, are you happy?"

I turned to stare at the old man.

"Happy?" I didn't understand the question.

"Yes. Happy."

"I…I don't know what you mean," I stammered uncertainly.

"I thought not." He turned away.

I continued to stare at him.

One of our group coughed a warning and I turned to see a figure in a white robe, approaching from the hospital on the West side of the property.

We immediately turned and those still seated got to their feet, preparatory to being escorted to our day's labours. As the figure grew closer, it separated itself into two persons, Master and Young Master.

Master glanced over all of us and inquired as to our health. Then he nodded to Meg, who had also risen at his approach. He motioned with his hand for two of the females to follow him to his building.

What they did there was unclear, but as they had red, work worn hands similar to Meg's, I assumed that they cleaned. Jack joined them. As I watched Master walking straight and stiff, I wondered, not for the first time, what his life was like.

In my younger years, I had often commented on the lack of difference in appearance between the Workers and the Masters. To my untrained eyes, the only difference between us was the colour of our clothing. When I first made this observation, I was immediately silenced by my instructor and told never to make such a comment again. This did not stop my thinking, however, though I was careful to keep such thoughts to myself thereafter.

Master and his group lived together in the huge white building on the south side of the property. Master had a female partner, named Mistress, and there were three others who lived with them, Young Master and two younger females.

The youngest was still a young-one and the fact that she stayed in Master's building instead of with all the other young-ones was a concept that was hard for me to understand. The other female was past the age of growing, but she did not work with us. She also spent her time in Master's building.

Young Master was a few seasons older than I and he already had the bearing and demeanour suitable to be a Master. Master had placed him in sole charge of the farm business some three years ago, and we were all accustomed to his presence, though sometimes I would find his eyes on me and a strange feeling would come over me. It was hard to understand and I would always try to dismiss it from my mind. It made me uncomfortable.

Now Young Master raised a white-garbed arm and pointed towards the south and Ross collected his five male workers, and started towards the fields. The rest of us divided up. Mia, a second female, and two other males, moved off towards the sewing and laundering rooms, which occupied a building near where my office was located. Another male and four females made their way towards the gardens. Hilary, recently come to us from the Growing buildings and also assigned to keep the accounts, and myself, were escorted into the main office to return to our huge ledgers and tomes.

Young Master moved past us to the east windows, unsealing them and swinging them wide. He performed the same procedure on the west windows alongside the door. The north and south windows he left, as the cooling breezes came from the east. He glanced around once more and then left.

Hilary and I went to our respective desks and sat down, preparatory to beginning our work. Without glancing up, I reached for my main ledger, but my hand only touched the polished surface of the desk. In surprise I looked up and realised that the huge volume was not where I had placed it—where I always placed it. It had been moved over to the other side of the desk and my smaller report book lay in its place.

"Someone has been in here," I said to Hilary. She glanced up in surprise. It was one of very few times that I had spoken to her, and certainly the sound of a human voice was always startling, but what I had said was impossible.

The buildings were always securely locked. We watched as the doors and windows were checked and sealed every night. We had just seen Young Master remove the seal from the door as he let us in. I stood up and moved quickly to the door.

Young Master was already halfway across the green. I had no way to get his attention, my virtually unused voice could never produce the volume to reach him if I called. I had to follow him. With a wildly beating heart, I started to run.

Young Master saw me just as he reached the far side of the compound. He turned towards me, a frown gathering on his brow. I knew the punishment for being out of place could be severe, but I felt he had to be told. He stopped and I panted up to him.

My body, although in good health, was not accustomed to such brisk exercise, and it was some seconds before I could tell him what the matter was. During that time, I felt his eyes on me, and I dared not look up.

As my breath finally came easier, he crossed his arms and said, "Speak."

"Young Master," I panted, "someone has been in the office and moved my books." I chanced a glimpse of his face when I had finished speaking and was surprised at the alarm that I read there. Without speaking, he took off towards the office. I followed as quickly as I could. As I entered the building moments later, he was standing beside my desk.

"What was disturbed?" he asked, not looking at me.

"My ledger and my smaller record book," I said. "I have not checked further."

"You are sure."

"Very sure. I always place my ledger on the right and my record book on my left. They were switched."

He turned slowly and looked carefully around the room. Suddenly he strode over to the small south window with an exclamation. Over his shoulder I could see the reason for his outburst. The window was simply hanging by the hinges, which ran across the top. It wasn't fastened in any way and moved easily when he pushed on it. He turned and his booted feet pounded loudly on the bare wood floor as he raced outside. I took my usual place, but folded my hands in my lap and did not touch anything.

Through all this, Hilary had kept her head down and appeared to work. But I knew now, as her eyes met mine that it had all been pretence. She could not help but be affected by what had happened and was as curious as I.

It wasn't long before Young Master returned, and Master with him. I scrambled to my feet and backed away from the desk.

"Have you touched anything?" Master asked me in a breathless voice.

"No, Master," I said quickly, careful to keep my eyes on his mouth as I spoke. He had beads of sweat standing out on his upper lip. I could feel something strange—fear?

"Go through your ledger and see if anything is disturbed...or missing," he said.

I resumed my seat, conscious of their eyes as I pulled my ledger over to me.

I leafed through it as rapidly as I could, trying to remember what receipts and notations I had received too late yesterday to have been entered in the record yet. "There are at least two of the receipts missing," I told him, shivering at the tension in the air. "But none of the notes and statements are gone that I can remember."

"What receipts!" His voice was raised almost to a shout by this time, and the unusual noise hurt my ears.

"Both are for goods delivered to the museum," I said, as evenly as I could. "There was one for supplies received yesterday morn, and another for a painting that same afternoon."

Master rubbed his forehead. I felt a distinct shock as I realised that his hand was shaking. "Receipts…receipts," he murmured distractedly. "What could he possibly want with receipts?"

"We'll discuss this, Father," said Young Master, putting a hand on Master's shoulder and urging him towards the door. "Come."

"One moment." He looked briefly back at me. "Check through everything else. See if something is amiss." They stood silently behind me and watched as I went through the two drawers of the desk and my record book.

"There's nothing else missing or disturbed that I can see right now," I told them.

"Continue with a more exact search and report your findings," Master said, his voice beginning to return to normal. "Carry on." They stepped outside and moved away from the door.

I looked at Hilary and caught her eye. She shrugged and turned back to her desk. I flipped several pages in the huge ledger and reached for a pen, preparatory to beginning work. As my shaking fingers touched the pen, however, it rolled away and fell to the floor. I stood up and walked around my desk to retrieve it. This brought me near the side window of our plain room, and as I knelt to find the pen, the voices of Young Master and Master came to me distinctly.

I glanced quickly up to see if Hilary had noticed my actions, but her back was turned and she appeared absorbed in what she was doing, so I stayed where I was.

Young Master was speaking. "We don't know that it was Ryley," he said quietly, obviously trying to soothe Master. "All we have is the obvious break-in…and our suspicions."

"Yes, you're right." Master's voice sounded tired. "We have no proof at all. But I know he is behind it."

34

"But what I don't understand is…" Young Master began.

"What?" Master prodded.

"Well there is absolutely no way Ryley could have gotten to the centre of the compound without *someone* seeing *something*!"

"What are you suggesting?" Master asked.

"That it seems more likely that…" again, Young Master paused.

"What!" Master was becoming impatient.

"Well it would be nearly impossible for someone to breach the perimeter, walk through the inner compound guards, break in here, and get out again, unless they were from inside, or had help from inside," Young Master said. There was silence for several seconds. "It wouldn't be the first time something like this had happened," he added.

"But not to us, Son!" Master said. "I don't even know how to handle something like this!"

"We'll just have to keep a closer watch—on everyone," Young Master said.

"Until we have something we can take to the Council," Master said.

"You insist that this is the work of Ryley, don't you?" Young Master said.

"Always, he has opposed me on the council. I know for a fact that he has plotted and schemed for my position for years. Until someone shows me proof of something different, I will continue to suspect his involvement," Master said.

"If we tried to take charges against Ryley to the council, we would look totally ridiculous!" Young Master said. "We'd be hissed out of the chambers! All we can prove is that he is making an effort to discredit you." He paused. "Even now, all we can do is wait until he, or someone, tries something further and be ready if they do."

"You're right," said Master, sounding tired, spent. "We must post more guards for the night-time hours. Take care of it." Silence. Young Master must have nodded because Master said, "Good."

"Now to further business," Master went on. "That young female who does my accounts. What is her name?"

A pause, then, "I believe you called her Listen, but I have heard the workers call her Liss."

"She is almost of the age of carrying, is she not?"

"She will soon reach her 21st year."

"As soon as she reaches the anniversary date, arrange to have her taken to the healer so he can judge the best time for her to enter the hospital."

"I am not sure that it should be done so soon, Father. I am afraid her small frame will not carry well."

"She will be given her chances regardless. If she has trouble, she will be sold. I cannot feed any non-producers. When the females reach their twenty-first year, they must begin the process or they will go."

"She is an exception because of her gift for numbers," Young Master argued. "She would be hard to replace."

"She will have four years here no matter what the outcome. During that time, see to it that we have another worker in the Growing buildings being fitted for her duties, just in case. I cannot change my rules for anyone."

"I…I will see to it, Father." They had begun to move away from the window and these last words were quite faint.

I realised that I had been crouching there on the floor for several minutes and that Hilary was looking curiously in my

36

direction. She could not have heard the quiet voices, so she could only put her own meaning upon my actions—perhaps she attributed my behaviour to the unusual and stressful events of the morning. I stood up, rather stiffly, clutching my pen in my hand, and returned to my desk.

I could not, at that time, put a name to what I was experiencing. Suffice it to say that there were many sensations warring with each other in my mind.

Fear was uppermost. I knew that I would soon be witness to events that were totally foreign to anything else in my existence thus far and the thought made me weak with trepidation. But I was feeling a bit of curiosity also. I was insatiably curious and this was just one more opportunity to feed that hunger.

Present also were those feelings that were so hard for me to comprehend. When Young Master spoke, I felt somehow warmed. I could not understand it. But I enjoyed it. None of my life's experiences had prepared me for it. He had actually defended me. I had never heard of that happening to any worker. My thoughts were in a turmoil.

I placed my own welfare and confusing feelings in the background to allow myself to concentrate on the first half of the conversation I had just overheard. I vaguely remembered Young Master using the term 'Father' once before, as he carried me to the hospital, and I felt heat rise to my cheeks as I realised that he must have been addressing Master and that Master had witnessed the whole spectacle.

I shook my head and rubbed my cheeks absently. Much of the rest of their conversation could not be understood. I had no idea who 'Ryley' was or why the Master was so upset over the disappearance of some receipts. His books were always very accurate and up-to-date. I saw to that personally. I did not see how discredit could be brought upon him. I decided to wait and watch for anything unusual. In an operation such as Master's, such events would be easily distinguished from the usual routine.

I would see.

CHAPTER FIVE

The day progressed normally from there on. Our midday meal was brought to us and we ate as we worked. No unusual activity could be discerned outside. The regular sounds of the workers filtered in through the open windows—someone directing one of the others in the garden. The neigh of one of Ross' horses as they worked the fields.

I worked a little more slowly than I normally did. The long columns seemed to blur before me and my mind wandered. But still I managed to finish the day's assigned labours just before Young Master came to collect us and return us to our rooms.

As we straightened our desks for the night, I felt his scrutiny and turning, caught his eye. I quickly dropped my gaze, but he seemed not to notice and stepped out of the office and strode quickly towards the Stable, not even looking to see if we followed. Upon reaching the courtyard, Young Master turned abruptly and went off towards Master's house, leaving us to take a small measure of leisure time in the cool evening air.

Looking about me, I could see that Ross and his crew had had a hot and dusty day. Their faces were streaked with dirt and their uniforms were badly stained with perspiration. Harry and his group looked like they had spent the day in the bright spring sunshine. Despite the hats that were provided with their tools, their skin had definitely been touched by the sun. Mia sat on the ground and rubbed her back. The bending that was a part of her work must have caused an ache that needed to be massaged away. Meg came out and sat near me. Glancing around, I moved a little closer to her.

"Meg, my time of carrying is coming," I said quietly, barely moving my lips and not looking at her.

She did not turn but she sighed deeply and answered, just as quietly, "I knew that it was getting closer."

"What do I do?"

"Nothing. There's nothing you can do. You must wait and do as you're told."

"Will I feel pain?"

"No, you will be asleep. They will give you something that will make you sleep, and when you awaken, it will be all done. Then you wait to see if you have caught."

"I'm afraid."

"Don't be. You will be fine."

"But I am small - perhaps too small to carry."

She turned and looked at me in surprise. "Where did you hear of such a thing?" she asked.

"I...I just thought of it," I lied.

She looked closely into my face. "Someone has said this to you," she said. "Pay no mind. You will be fine." She arose and placed her hands in the small of her back, stretching as she did so. She glanced quickly about, then she turned to me and laid her hand on my shoulder. I looked up at her and was surprised to see water welling up in those dark eyes.

She shook her head and sighed again. Then she walked slowly back into the cooking area of the stables.

Jack had apparently been dozing near her but now he looked at me, his eyes glittering strangely in the dusk. "They're going to start on you, now," he said. "Well I'll have something to say about it." He rose and moved towards his room.

The rest of us remained sitting, silent, relaxed and lost in our thoughts, until the bell sounded for the second and last time of the day. Then we stood and filed into the building, each leaving the group as it passed our individual doors. Yetta or Meg had placed a

40

tray of food in each of our rooms and there was also another pitcher of warm water at hand.

I closed the door and washed my hands, scrubbing at the ink blotches which were always present at the end of my day. Drying them on a cloth, I glanced at the tray.

Master had always felt that good food made a healthy worker, so there was always ample, but not excess. Tonight was no exception. There were long white parsnips and some potatoes, still in their skin. There was squash and red beets. For a sweet, I saw an orange and two plums. Alongside was a thick slice of fresh bread and a tall glass of cool milk.

But there was something different tonight. A thin slice of the flesh of an animal was tucked in under the potatoes. I pulled it out and looked at it closely. I hadn't tasted meat before, but I knew about it and had glimpsed it on other trays when I had chanced to be in the doorway as Yetta passed. Its presence on my tray told me that I was truly being prepared for carrying. For a few minutes, my mind seemed to freeze over and I simply stood there, staring at the meat in my hand. Finally, I tried to brush the thoughts aside sat down to my meal.

The events of the day and the conversation I had overheard had affected my appetite and I found I could eat little of what had been brought. I managed to swallow a small portion of everything, and was surprised at the taste and texture of the meat, but my usual enjoyment was missing and I set the almost untouched tray beside the door for Yetta and prepared for bed. I could hear the usual routine going on all about me. The collection of the trays, Ross' crew being escorted to the toilet building for their evening wash, workers settling for the night - closing doors and opening windows.

I was surprised by a soft tap at my door—usually, Yetta simply opened it wide enough to retrieve the tray, then disappeared—and Meg slipped in. She walked over to where I was laying and crouched down beside my pallet.

I sat up.

"What are your thoughts?" she asked, softly.

"The events of the morning are going around and around in my head, but I am uncertain about the coming events in my own future," I answered. "And I am very confused."

"I have heard what happened this morning. It does not concern us. What I want to talk to you about is your time of carrying. Your confusion is to be understood," she whispered. "I, too felt the same way four years ago, before my first operation."

"I am also a little curious," I confessed, not looking at her. "Is that usual?"

"I only know of my own experience," she said softly. "And I felt no curiosity. But you are different from me, from all of us. You want to know everything. You're always listening to everyone. Oh, no, don't think I haven't noticed," she said when I would have protested, ashamed that everyone seemed to know my deepest secret.

"You are different from the rest of us," she repeated. "You want to know things. You are of a new order and you are our future."

"It is for that reason that you will be leaving tonight."

I was struck dumb with horror. My heart seemed to freeze and contract within me. All my life, I had imagined being sent to another Master and I had known fear, but never had I imagined *such* fear. I felt like I was collapsing, that I would shrink and wither through panic as Jack had through age.

Meg must have seen my thoughts in my eyes. "No, no," she whispered quickly. "You haven't been sold. You won't be leaving to go to another farm. Jack is going to take you away."

Some of the terror that filled my heart was stilled. I looked at her. "How...?" I tried again, "How can this be so?" I was almost afraid I had misunderstood. Where could we go? What places were there except for other farms?

Panic began to build again as I thought of the extensive records for each worker that Hilary was in charge of and that I had often stolen a peek into. Information collected as to description, habits, talents. It would be impossible for two workers to go anywhere without someone finding and returning them. The thought of possible repercussions was almost too much for even my imagination.

"Jack knows of a place that he thinks will be safe still," Meg said quietly. "A people from the Before Times who, because of their location, were sheltered and preserved. He wants to take you to them."

I looked at her. "Don't they keep records of their workers? Wouldn't they send us back?"

"I know this will be hard for you to understand," she said, looking toward the window. "But they have no workers. Everyone lives like Master."

I lay back, frowning and tried to visualise what it would be like. Me, with hundreds, maybe thousands, of Masters.

I could only imagine an early death.

Meg rose to her feet, glancing once more at the fading light glowing softly through my tiny window. "Jack will be here as soon as it is dark," she said. "You will need your clothes and necessities. We will provide the rest." She walked slowly towards the door and picked up my tray.

"Meg," I asked, "Are you coming?"

She paused briefly, then went out quietly and closed the door. She wasn't. But it was then that I knew that she wanted to.

I did not know what to think. This was the only life I had known. I could not picture working for any other master and certainly could not imagine serving more than one. I felt my life was indeed over.

CHAPTER SIX

The evening wore on and I used the time to advantage. I carefully folded all my clothing and stuffed it inside one of my uniforms along with my comb and the small brush I used to clean my teeth. I added my blanket, for I didn't know what my situation would be and what needs I would have to meet myself. My boots, I would wear, and I was grateful that this would prevent me from having their heavy weight on my back.

I fastened the uniform and tied each arm to its corresponding leg, so I could sling it on my back like a pack. Then I turned out my light and lay down on my pallet to wait.

The night was still and I could hear the sounds of the tiny creatures, whose rustlings were hidden by louder noises during the day. There was a bright moon and I watched its light shift direction through my window, much as the sun had only this morning.

Just as I was becoming drowsy, I became aware of other sounds—footsteps and large bodies moving about. I stood up and realised by the movement of air that my door was opening slowly. My heart began to beat very quickly and I put my hand over it to muffle the sound. I was sure it could be heard across the whole property.

Meg crept into the room. "Follow me," she whispered almost soundlessly.

I got shakily to my feet. Reaching out, I grasped a handful of her uniform and, clutching my makeshift pack in my other hand, moved quietly out of the room behind her.

Meg proceeded along the hallway for several paces, then stopped. I peered owlishly around her and could dimly make out the outline of someone standing just inside the outer door. He

45

moved and I recognised Jack. He turned and softly opened the door. I released my hold of Meg and followed. I could feel someone moving behind me, and thinking it was Meg and that she would be coming after all, I turned to speak to her. I could see no one, but the sounds continued and I knew that someone followed.

As we stepped quietly out into the moonlight, I realised with relief, that it was Ross who followed and that the darkness of his skin had prevented me from seeing him. To my surprise, Mia stepped out behind him. Her dark skin, too, was extremely difficult to see in the dim light. Both of them had huge, black blankets thrown about their shoulders that hung almost to the ground and hid the blue of their uniforms. Looking down, I could see that this was wise, because in the darkness, my uniform looked almost as white as a master's robe.

Ross stepped close to me and threw another blanket around me, holding the front closed until I could adjust my load and take hold myself. I was instantly assailed by an unknown smell, which seemed to be emanating from the folds of the rough cloth. I knew without being told that Ross had brought us several blankets usually used to cover Master's horses and that those same blankets had captured the smell of the sweat and dust that were farming.

Ross handed a fourth blanket to Jack and he covered himself, moving silently up the hill towards Master's house as he did so. We followed, careful to make no sound.

The path that Jack had chosen led right past the huge white building, and with each step we took, it looked a little taller—as if it were growing and would soon reach right into the clouds. The beating of my heart seemed deafening in the stillness and I was certain it would awaken everyone.

We moved around the house to the north and west and had just reached the deep shadows behind, when the door on the south end of the building opened and the heavy steps of several pairs of boots clumped slowly down the stairway.

At first, I figured Master or Young Master were starting out to check on something and I felt a pricking of doom as I thought of being missed…or being found. Then as they drew nearer, I realised that each of them was dressed in a lightly coloured uniform. I drew in a breath or relief. I had forgotten about the guard that Master had ordered placed at the office. These must be the workers who had been assigned. I guessed that they had just received their instructions.

We flattened ourselves against the ground and waited. The workers moved, silent, as always, towards the office and I was grateful that it was on the opposite side of Master's property from where we were hidden. The sound of their passage faded and I breathed easier.

But Jack did not relax. I could see his heavily seamed face as he looked up towards the windows of the darkened house above us. "Someone in there has to be awake," he whispered. "How do we know where they are. What if they chance to look out just as we start up the slope? When we're exposed." He looked down at me. "I don't know what to do," he said heavily.

I turned my body so I, too could look up at the house. "If someone sent those men out to guard, would it not be more logical for them to be looking towards the office?" I asked. "That is where the concern is."

"You're right," said Jack. "We cannot wait any longer, anyway. We must chance it." He got to his feet, though he remained in a hunched position and, taking a new grip on his blanket covering, started up the large slope.

The other two followed closely and I brought up the rear.

I found juggling my bundle and holding my blanket to be awkward and halfway up the slope, I stopped to readjust my load. As I did so, I chanced to look back at the darkened windows of the house. Something white moved in the bottom right-hand pane and I froze, feeling the shock reach the ends of my fingers and toes.

Someone was there. As I watched, the face moved into the meagre light and I recognised Young Master. He didn't move, just looked at me, and for a long minute, I looked back at him. Suddenly, my heart felt heavy, as if it laboured with difficulty in the simple performance of its duty.

Why did we have to leave? What was so terrible here? My eyes felt strange—prickly—and I lifted my hand to rub them. I felt moisture and realised that they were leaking water—as I had seen Jack's and Meg's do. What was wrong with me? I drew my sleeve across my eyes and looked once more at the face dimly visible in the window. Young Master raised his hand, as though he would beckon to me, but then he simply rested his fingers against the glass.

Slowly, I turned away. Climbing the slight incline suddenly became work, my body felt clumsy, weighted. Resolutely, I moved, half hoping to hear Young Master's voice, fearful of hearing the sound of the alarm instead.

But the silence continued and the only sounds I heard were those made by the workers toiling ahead of me. I paused to look back now and then. Young Master remained where he was, watching us. When I reached the top, I turned for one last glimpse.

He was no longer looking at me, though he remained where he was. He seemed to have bent his head and was resting his forehead against the glass of the window. Then the hill hid him from my sight.

CHAPTER SEVEN

Jack and the others had stopped and I soon caught up to them. I looked at them curiously, wondering why they stood there. Then I realised they were looking at something. I turned and gasped.

We were facing the largest building I had ever seen. In the light of the moon, its white walls appeared almost unreal—part of a featureless blob floating above the ground. Somehow, I knew that this was the 'museum', which I had long heard of and kept records for. I had known it was somewhere on Master's property, but now that I could finally look at it, its mere size almost rendered me incapable of moving.

Jack tugged on my blanket, and when he had finally gathered my attention, he indicated that I should again follow him.

We moved once more in single file across a white road and into a small patch of trees. There, Jack signalled for us to stop and rest. He dropped the black horse blanket and set a bundle down on the ground.

I recognised the familiar blue cloth and realised that he had constructed a pack for his necessities out of one of his blankets.

He untied it and threw back one side to reveal its contents. I gasped as I recognised the white material from which a master's robes are constructed. He grasped a handful of the white folds and withdrew four garments.

"Where did you get these?" I asked, hardly daring to touch the soft cloth.

"Mia supplied them from the laundry," he said, touching her shoulder briefly. "She has been collecting them for some time, preparing for this night."

"You all knew this was going to happen?" I asked, squinting to see their faces.

"Oh, we knew we wanted to try it," Jack replied. "We just didn't know when."

"But why do we want to leave?" I asked, some of my confusion becoming apparent. "Why don't we like it here?"

The other three looked at each other and then silently stood up and started to pull the robes on over their uniforms.

With some misgivings, I rose and did the same.

We folded the dark blankets and left them under the trees. Jack retied his bundle and slung it over his shoulder. I did the same with my pack and Ross and Mia picked up their bundles.

We were ready, though I didn't know what we were ready for.

Jack again led the way and we filed silently out of the trees and onto the hard white road leading to the entrance of the museum. This time, Jack followed the road and as we drew closer to the building, I could see two huge wooden doors shut tight against the night. Erect and unafraid, Jack walked right up to the doors and knocked several times, quickly and in a regular pattern.

After some time, we could hear footsteps approaching from inside and the clank of metal as someone began to unseal the door. Suddenly there was a large click and the door began to swing inwards. A pale light shone through the opening and we quickly moved into the light and out of the cool, dark night. The smell of stale air met us as we entered, and I turned to see who had provided entrance.

A small worker was pushing the door shut and resealing the chains and locks. By size, I figured her to be a young-one. As she turned and picked up a lantern from the floor, I realised that she was old—probably as old as Jack himself—and as withered and shrunken as a plant left too long without water.

Her hair though cut in the same style as my own, was a peculiar silver colour and her face was a netting of fine lines, making her skin look delicate and fragile as though it had been made of cobwebs. She looked at each of us carefully, her eyes seeming to linger the longest on me and finally turned to Jack.

Then the two of them did something that was at once strange and somehow beautiful. They put their arms around each other and simply held on tightly.

For no reason at all, I found myself thinking of Young Master. I glanced at Ross and Mia and saw that they were as confused as I. But we said nothing. Jack and the female soon released each other and Jack placed a gentle hand for a moment on her cheek, then he turned to us.

"This is Rachael," he said, simply. "I knew her in the Before Times."

Rachael stretched her mouth, showing nearly toothless gums and squeezed her eyes shut. We were uncertain how to respond, so we gave the two-fingered salute that was the only contact we knew.

She appeared to be satisfied. She turned to Jack. "The other workers are busy in the upper floors, so we shouldn't be noticed," she said. "But your robes will stop any questions if we are seen."

"Good," Jack said, "But we will still need to work quickly."

"Follow me," said Rachael. She led the way deeper into the museum, and I caught glimpses of huge metal creatures, still and silent, lining the walls on either side. "These are machines," said Jack, noticing our interest. "They were used to do most of the work in the Before Times."

I could not understand how these enormous creations could do the work that we workers did now, but I accepted his statements, hoping to examine the machines and appease some of my curiosity in the near future.

Jack and Rachael had reached a door similar to the one through which we had entered and Rachael proceeded to unseal it. While she worked, I took the opportunity to move towards the machine that stood closest to me.

It was enormous - fully three times higher than myself. It had four huge wheels - which alone stood taller than me - and a box-like affair that sat between the two back wheels and was simply a frame with windows. Joined to it in front and resting between the two front wheels was another box, this one larger and made of metal. It was yellow in colour, and had several slits along the side, almost like the vents built into the walls of some buildings. It had two smokestacks, which seemed to sprout out of the yellow part, but I could not see any place that would serve as a fire-box and figured that it must be deep inside the machine.

"Liss," Jack called quietly.

I left my exploring and ceased to puzzle over the use of such a creation as I realised that the doors were open and everyone was leaving. I followed and once again breathed great lungs full of the marvellous night air.

We were at the edge of a huge depression carved out of the land. Wooden steps down one side provided access to the bottom. Rachael, still carrying her lamp, started down.

Jack followed, gesturing for us to do the same. He spoke softly over his shoulder as we descended, "This is a box canyon. It provides a very private outdoor addition to the museum. Masters and their families come down here to enjoy the sunshine in the park without worrying about who can see them. It is almost completely cut off from the world—in fact, it is a little world in itself. The masters find great enjoyment here."

We had been moving deeper into the canyon for several moments when Rachael finally paused. "Be careful here," she said. "This is the last step."

We took her advice in negotiating the last few steps, and were relieved to feel the earth beneath our feet once again.

The darkness was almost thick here in the bottom of the canyon and the feeble light of the lantern was able to penetrate only a small portion of it. Soft grass stretched away on all sides as far as we could see and strange blossom-laden bushes seemed to sprout from the ground at regular intervals, scenting the air with spring. We followed Rachael and her lantern as she moved forward, skirting trees and making no sound in the soft grasses.

52

After a short period of time, I caught the glint of silver ahead. I strained my eyes in an attempt to see what was waiting for us in the darkness there. Soon Rachael stopped and held her lantern high. There, in its light, was the strangest sight I had ever seen.

A large metal bird gleamed dully in the light. It sat with wings outspread, almost as if it were soaring already. As we walked around it, I was surprised to see that it had no head. There was a twisted blade where the head should have gone. The feet, also were gone. Instead it rested on three black wheels. We completed a circle of it, reaching out with uncertain fingers to touch the smooth, cool skin and seeing what we could in the dim light, then we returned to Jack, who was waiting patiently beside Rachael.

"What is this?" asked Ross. "You said we would be leaving this place and now you bring us to this box in the earth and show us yet another of your machines. When…and how are we leaving?"

"I have not attempted to explain many things," Jack answered him quietly. "Because it would be too hard to do so with your limited knowledge. There is so much that you simply could not comprehend because it is so different from anything you have ever known." He looked up at the strange machine and touched the silvery skin reverently. "This machine is going to provide our freedom," he continued. "It flies."

We looked at him with what must have been blank amazement. No one could fly. We were simply not equipped as the birds were - to wheel and soar and disappear into the clouds. He had tricked us. There would be no new life, no change. We would go back to the Stable and, if we hadn't been discovered, attempt to perform a full day's labour with no sleep.

I had never felt this way before, like my life wasn't worth living. I could not understand myself. I didn't have the least idea why we wanted to leave, but now that it had become a possibility, there was nothing else that I wanted to do more.

There was also the distinct possibility that our absence had been noticed, and I shuddered to think of what the punishment would be. No one had ever tried to leave our Master before, but we had heard whispers from other farms, and the discipline in those places was almost more than I could picture.

We were stuck. I waited for Jack's next words.

He stretched his mouth, as Rachael had earlier and I saw that she was doing the same. "You must trust me," he said. "You have heard me speak of being a pilot?"

I frowned to myself—had I heard him mention it? I couldn't remember.

He went on, "Well this is what I piloted—or at least one similar to it. This is called a plane, an aeroplane."

He looked at us. "And it does fly, very well."

"The main reason that Master had me brought to his farm was because of my background," he added. "This plane was brought to the museum by one of the Masters, and as it was in such good shape, though it is over fifty years old, it was decided by the council that it should be restored to working condition."

"I didn't realise that my work with planes was so well known, but I guess it was included with my reports. These were forwarded to Master when the request for expertise went out, and here I am. For several weeks, I have been brought here every day to work on it. I finished it last week."

"Master is very thorough when he takes charge of anything," Jack went on. "He even brought in containers of fuel from who knows where so I could be sure the engine was working properly. At first he brought in several cases of the wrong type of fuel, but I could see that they, too might come in handy, so I had them stored on board, telling him that they were also a necessity. I played one other little trick on him also - I greatly exaggerated the amount of gas I would need, so we have enough to go a great distance."

Jack turned towards us. "But now we must work. I must ask you to trust me a little longer. I can explain more clearly when we are away from here. Dawn is at hand and we must be ready as soon as it is light enough to see."

Jack told us that our first duty was to clear the bushes and tall plants from a straight path ahead and behind the machine. Ross, Mia and I moved around to the front and began uprooting the fragrant plants and throwing them off to the side.

Something touched my arm and I glanced up, startled.

Rachael was standing beside me, her eyes on my face.

I straightened and looked at her.

She placed two soft, worn hands on either side of my face and simply stood there, looking into my eyes. Then she dropped her hands and stepped back.

I stared at her a moment longer, then, as she turned away, bent to my work once more.

It was hard work and Ross and Mia were a good deal better at it than I, but as the sky began to lighten, we could see that we had worked well and were nearly finished. As Ross pulled up the last of the bushes, Mia and I walked back to the plane to begin work behind it.

Jack was busily opening containers and pouring liquid into a small hole in the side of the plane. The smell as we approached was not unpleasant, but certainly different. Rachael's lantern was sitting on the ground, far enough from him that its light was almost useless, and Rachael had disappeared.

"Where is Rachael?" I asked him, looking about, "Is she not coming?"

"She cannot," he replied briefly and as he looked up at me, I was surprised to see two wet tracks which stained his cheeks and ran down his face. He quickly brushed them away and stooped again to his work.

I frowned briefly, not understanding and finally walked around him and began to pull up the few plants and shrubs that were directly behind the plane. Moving in this direction, the work took very little time and we were almost finished by the time Ross joined us.

Jack called to us. "We must leave now," he said. "It is light enough for me to navigate, but also light enough to easily be discovered if we wait."

We ran over to the plane and picked up our bundles, waiting for his next instructions.

Jack reached up and grasped a metal lever which protruded from the side of the machine and turned it. A line in the skin suddenly became a door and he swung it wide. Then he reached in and pulled out a small set of stairs, which were attached to the inner wall of the plane. He gestured for me to go first and with a good deal of fear, and an equal amount of curiosity, I climbed the few steps and stepped inside.

There was not enough room for a normal sized person to stand fully, though I had little trouble. There were six very strange-looking chairs with soft lines and cloth covering them completely. In front of the foremost two, there were two frames attached to a wall. The lower half of the wall as well as the ceiling directly overhead was covered with little knobs, levers, wheels, and buttons. The upper half contained two large windows which curved around to the sides.

Mia pushed in behind me and I moved forward, choosing for myself the front seat on the left. Mia and Ross sat directly behind me and Jack climbed in, folded the stairs and swung the door shut.

"You must give me your bundles," he said. As we handed them to him, he carefully placed them inside a very tiny cubicle in the wall of the plane opposite the door. He closed the opening tightly, then he moved to the front.

"Liss, you are going to have to move to the other chair here," he said, looking down at me. "Unless of course you want to make this bird fly." I was quick to shift my body into the opposite seat and I watched as he lowered himself slowly into the one I had left.

56

Jack was tired. I had forgotten his extreme age and how hard it was for him to keep up with the rest of us.

"Are you able to work?" I asked him as he sat for a moment with his eyes closed.

"I'm fine, Liss," he answered. "I'm just having a prayer before my flight."

"A prayer?"

"Something else I will explain to you when we have the time." Jack flipped several of the levers and pushed some buttons, thumping with his knuckles when something didn't perform as it was supposed to. Then he looked at me and asked, "Ready?"

I couldn't speak. I nodded.

He showed each of us how to fasten the belts that were attached to our chairs and then he turned another lever and the machine began making noises.

At first, it sounded like the loud beating of a quail's wings, but then it began to make a noise that was impossible to speak over. A loud roar, as of thunder crashing constantly. I put my hands over my ears and, glancing back, saw that Ross and Mia had done the same.

Jack grasped the framework in front of him and twisted it to the left and I was startled to see the similar framework before me move at the same time. I reached out to touch it, but Jack gestured for me to leave it be, so I settled back into my seat once more and again covered my ears.

The plane moved, jerking forward suddenly and I grabbed for the sides of my chair as I felt it. Too fascinated to be frightened, I looked out the window closest to me and watched as we turned until we were facing opposite to our original direction and then we again began to move forward. When the machine reached the side of the canyon near the stairs, it again turned around so that it was once more facing the far wall.

As it turned this last time, I saw that several workers had come out of the museum and were standing atop the stairway. But another sight filled me with horror. A master was halfway down the stairs and descending rapidly, moving his mouth and waving his arms.

"We must leave quickly!" I said to Jack, my voice filled with panic.

He pushed forward on a thick metal stick beside him on the floor, and we began to move toward the far wall. Faster and faster, the plane went until it was moving so fast that I couldn't feel the wheels bouncing any more. I looked out my window and realised that I couldn't feel the ground because we were no longer *on* the ground. We were indeed flying, as Jack had promised.

The excitement I felt dissolved, however, when I looked up at the side of the canyon directly in front of us and knew that we were not high enough to rise above it and that we could never stop in time to avoid hitting it.

Just as our death seem inevitable, I noticed a small crack in the great wall of rock. We were moving directly towards it. It seemed tiny, too tiny to allow the passage of the machine in which I sat. But as it grew closer, I realised that Jack was indeed going to pilot his plane directly into it. I threw my arms over my head and waited to hear my last sounds on earth.

The rhythm of the plane did not change and there was no abrupt halt or sound of metal and rock meeting, so I slowly withdrew my arms and glanced cautiously out. Jack had safely guided his machine into the seemingly tiny crack and we were out of the canyon.

He looked over at me and again stretched his mouth. "I wasn't just a pilot," he said. "I was a great pilot."

CHAPTER EIGHT

For some time, he followed the crack, which seemed to stretch for miles and grew ever wider. Then he pulled back on the framework, which he still clutched and we were suddenly sailing far above the ground.

The sun was rising in the east and the sky was cloudless. Everywhere we looked, the land was touched with gold. Much of it was bare, with only grasses covering it, and seamed with huge cracks, similar to the one which had led out of the canyon. I caught glimpses of other farms nestled right in some of them as we passed.

We flew over many settlements built right out in the open, much the same as Master's and I could see the tiny specs that were the workers in fields and gardens as we flew over. I wondered what they thought when they heard us, or even if they could.

I saw a group of buildings clustered together beside a large field of water which Jack said was a lake. He told me that such a settlement was called a town and that several masters lived in one place and had their lands around the outside. That way they could work together and help each other. I knew that Ross and his crew had worked together and that Emily's group had done the same, but it was hard for me to imagine what it would be like to work with someone. To co-operate and combine effort.

Always, I had worked alone.

I glanced over at Jack, a question on my lips, but closed my mouth abruptly when I saw that he was gazing intently out towards the right side of the plane, his face puckered and furrowed.

My eyes followed his.

Several structures, grouped closely together had come into view. Another settlement. I stared at it. There was something different about it.

At first, I thought it was the height of the buildings, for some of them rivalled and even surpassed Master's great museum.

Then I realized that these buildings, though certainly tall, looked unfinished or . . . broken off. Their upper stories thrust jaggedly into the clear air.

Like . . . bones.

I stared down as we flew over. Nothing moved. "What is this place?" I asked Jack.

He turned his face towards the front of the plane.

"Just another settlement," he said.

I looked out of the window again. "It isn't like the others," I said finally.

"No, you're right, Liss," he said. "It isn't like the others."

I waited for him to go on, but after a few minutes, it was obvious that he had said all he wanted to.

"But what settlement is it?" I asked, finally. "Why are those building unfinished? Is it just being built?"

He sighed. "They're not unfinished, Liss," he said patiently. "They've been destroyed."

The settlement had disappeared behind us, but I looked back towards where I had last seen it. "Destroyed?"

"It is one of the cities that was ruined in the war," he said. "No one lives there now."

"So it is from the Before Times," I said, mostly to myself.

"Yes."

I could see that he was unwilling to talk about it. "You would rather not discuss it?" I asked him.

He reached out and patted my hand. "You need to know, Liss," he said. "But I think I need time."

I nodded.

We flew for some time and slowly, some of the fear and excitement drained from my body, leaving me suddenly sleepy. Jack looked over at me. "Tired?" he asked briefly. I nodded. "Lean back and rest, if you can, Liss," he said. "This will be a long flight." Obediently, I sat back in my chair and was soon asleep.

How long I slept, I do not know, but when I awoke, the rhythm of the plane had changed and it felt as though I was rising from my seat. Checking my belt, I discovered that I was still tightly fastened into my chair. Then glancing out the window, I realised that we were sinking towards the ground.

I looked at Jack, a question on my lips, but he had been watching me and spoke even as I opened my mouth. "We have to set down for a few minutes so I can refuel, Liss," he said. "Don't worry. There isn't anything wrong and I passed the last settlement several minutes ago, so we shouldn't be interrupted."

I accepted his words and relaxed into my chair again.

Looking out the window, I watched as the trees and bushes below seemed to grow larger with each passing second. I realised that they were simply getting closer. Soon, I could feel the wheels under us bump along the ground and I knew that we were flying no longer.

Jack had landed in a very barren spot. There were a few scrubby bushes and one or two trees, but mostly the ground was covered by short, fuzzy-looking grass. Jack rose out of his seat. "You may want to stretch your legs for a while," he said over his shoulder as he moved towards the door of the machine. I quickly unbuckled my belt and followed him. Ross and Mia were talking quietly together, and I left them where they were.

Jack had opened the door and was pushing the steps outside when I joined him. He poked his head out and looked around. "Nothing to be afraid of here," he said and moved aside to let me descend. Then he disappeared towards the back of the plane. I craned my neck and leaned on the stairway in an effort to see what he was doing.

He had opened a small door in the very back of the plane's interior and was pulling out containers. They were similar to those with which he had been working just before we had left the canyon, and I knew that they must contain the fuel that was so necessary for this bird to fly.

I caught a glimpse of other crates and boxes neatly stored in the space, but these, Jack did not touch. I straightened up and turned around, letting my eyes wander over the countryside.

I was struck by the emptiness of it all. Nothing moved. No animals, no birds, and certainly no workers or masters. It was quiet, and I felt a sudden and very strong urge to be with…someone. I shook my head and walked out onto the plain a little way, kicking at the dusty ground and rubbing my feet along the dry, odd-looking grass.

Behind me, I could hear Jack busy with his containers and soon I caught a whiff of the fuel. Abruptly, I turned and almost ran into Ross and Mia. They had followed me and were standing just behind me gazing at the view. Mia carried a sack in one arm, and she held it toward me.

"Something to eat, Liss?" she asked shyly.

"I thank you, no," I said quietly. "I do not have any appetite right now."

She lowered her arms and nodded. Ross was eating something, and he finished whatever it was and reached into the bag for more.

I left them and walked back to the plane. Jack was still pouring liquid into a little hole in the side of our bird and the smell was quite strong.

"Can I help somehow?" I asked. Always I had had my own work to do and had never had the time – or felt the need – to help anyone. But my job had been left behind, at Master's, and I was feeling my inactivity.

"I fear that this work is a little heavy for you," Jack said, "But you could call Ross over here."

I turned and called to Ross and Mia and they walked quickly back to where we were standing.

Jack spoke briefly to Ross and handed him one of the containers. Ross' huge arms bulged as he lifted the heavy container and continued the job that Jack had started. I looked at Jack in wonder. Even now, he seemed so aged and frail and yet he was able to do a job that took great effort from a male much younger. His strength and agility belied his years.

As Ross finished with each container, he handed it to Mia and she stacked them neatly.

I walked over to where Jack had laid down on the ground nearby, and sat down beside him.

Ross continued to pour the liquid into the plane, wiping sweat from his brow with the sleeve of his white robe as he worked.

Jack's breathing became slow and even and I knew that he slept. I was glad to see him snatch even so brief a rest.

"What's that?" Mia's voice startled me and I looked up.

A cloud of dust was approaching from the south. At the base of it, I could just make out two or three tiny specks. For several seconds, we stared at it, unsure of what it was, or of what we should do about it.

"I don't know," Ross answered her. "Should we wake Jack?"

I looked down at the peaceful face beside me and sighed. "I don't want to," I said. "I want to let him rest."

"Well I'm not sure what that cloud of dust means," Ross said. "But back at Master's, a cloud like that usually meant that a herd of something was approaching." He narrowed his eyes. "Moving that fast, I would suspect horses."

He finished with the container he was using and, setting it down, walked over to where Jack rested. Leaning down, he shook Jack's shoulder.

Jack started awake at Ross' touch and rubbed a hand over his face. "Finished?" he asked, getting stiffly to his feet.

"Not quite," Ross said.

"Well, as soon as you are, we'll load the empty containers back into the cargo section and start out again," Jack said. He started towards the plane. "I guess we can—" he stopped in mid sentence, his eyes suddenly on the cloud of dust behind us.

"That's why we woke you," Ross said.

I turned around. The specks had grown large.

"Riders!" Jack said briefly. "Quickly, we must go!" He grabbed a container and shook it. Then setting it down, he picked up another.

"Did you empty all of them?" he asked, glancing at Ross.

"All but that one," Ross said, pointing.

Jack grabbed the full container and set it down close to the empty ones. Then he unscrewed the lid and tipped it on its side, allowing the strange-smelling liquid to pour out onto the dry grass.

"Everyone into the plane!" he said.

Ross pushed Mia before him up the steep stairs and the two of them disappeared. I followed them slowly, unwilling to leave Jack.

A strange 'popping' sound started and I glanced toward the riders just as something struck the ground beside me, raising a little puff of dust.

"Liss, hurry!" Jack said, urgently.

The popping sound came again. This time, several objects struck the steps, glancing off the ones just below and just above my feet. I stared at the gashes that appeared in the metal.

"Liss, they're shooting at you!" Jack screamed at me. "Get into the plane!"

I started up the steps, still wondering what was happening.

Ross appeared in the doorway and grabbed my shoulders, tossing me easily into the plane. Then he jumped to the ground and ran to Jack.

I pulled myself to my feet and turned to watch as the huge man lifted Jack in his arms. Jack dropped something just as Ross began to run towards the plane.

A ball of flame appeared suddenly where Jack had been standing only moments before and immediately engulfed the little collection of canisters.

Then Ross reached the stairs. As he leaped up them, there were some more pops.

Jack gasped, suddenly. Then Ross thrust him through the door and, turning, began to wrench at the stairway.

More popping. This time, whatever was being thrown at us came in through the door and bounced around inside the plane, making a terrible ringing sound.

Then I heard a huge explosion and, through the doorway, felt the heat of a dozen fireplaces as the windows on the stairway side lit with a brilliant orange glow.

Jack stumbled forward to his seat and dropped into it. Then he frantically began to press buttons and switches.

Ross had finally managed to pull the stairs into the plane and shut the door.

Outside, I could hear voices, shouting something unintelligible.

Then the sound of the plane coming to life drowned out everything else. Jack adjusted some more switches and pushed the lever on the floor forward.

Slowly we started to move.

I turned to look at the riders, but all I could make out was a great wall of fire, burning wildly and slowly falling behind as the plane began to go faster.

Some shadowy figures seemed to be milling about on the far side of it, but I couldn't see them clearly through the flames. I sank into my seat, just as the plane stopped bumping and I knew that the wheels had left the ground. Once more, we were headed into the sky.

The Riders fell far behind.

I turned to Jack, "Who were they?"

Jack didn't look at me. Instead, he kept his eyes on the window before him, and on the plane's controls. "Masters," he said, shortly.

"But how did they know where we were?" Suddenly, everything seemed futile. No matter what we did, no matter where we went, the Masters would find us.

"They must have been from one of the last settlements," Jack said. He coughed. "Now stop asking questions, Liss, I have to concentrate."

For several minutes, I watched him handle the controls. The plane went higher and higher.

Finally, Jack grunted in satisfaction and flipped a switch. "Now, we can relax for a moment," he said.

"Good. How long will it be till we get there?"

"We'll be a few hours, yet," he answered. "You relax and watch the scenery go by."

Obediently I turned my head and looked at the ground so far below. I watched it steadily for what seemed hours. Then my eyelids began to droop and slowly, I drifted again into slumber.

When I awoke, we were facing into a setting sun and heading toward what appeared to be an enormous blue wall on the horizon. Looking down out of my window, I saw that the flat land that I was used to had given way to hills that seemed to roll beneath us. Long grasses covered them -- rich growth that I had never before seen. I looked toward the uneven blue line ahead and wondered again just where Jack was taking us.

Glancing quickly behind me, I realised that Ross and Mia had succumbed to sleep and were still resting quietly. Jack continued to direct us to our destination, but he was hunched over his hands and I guessed that he was very tired.

"Is there something I can do?" I asked him. "You look as though your body could use some rest."

He coughed. "I am tired," he answered, his voice alarmingly weak. "But I will make it. We are almost there."

I quickly glanced out the window again, but the sight was very unsettling to me. I did not see any settlements, and the threatening, jutting wall kept coming closer. I looked at the shadow of the plane, now following a little behind us, and saw it slip silently over the landscape. It slid over a large group of trees, and something about them captured my attention.

They had not been planted in rows, but looked like they had been placed in a completely haphazard manner. "Jack, why are those trees planted in such a peculiar way?"

"Peculiar?"

"They do not follow any set pattern. They are not in correct rows."

"They weren't planted by workers or masters."

"But how did they get there?"

"They are one of the few things left from the Before Times. They grew there naturally. Their presence and that of those mountains ahead tell me that we are getting close to our people."

"Mountains. Is that what that great wall is called?"

"Great wall? Oh...oh, yes. I guess it does look like a wall. Actually, it is one of the most beautiful sights in this country—to me, anyway. This is one of the few places left that has been allowed to keep its natural state. Oh, the masters tried to penetrate this stronghold, but were unable to and the people who had taken refuge there were left alone."

"You mean your people built this?"

"No, no. These are one of the few natural wonders left in our world. They are great humps of rock pushed up from underneath."

"Did the war do that?"

"No, Liss. The war didn't do that. They were created when this world was created."

"I don't understand."

"You wil...you will."

The plane was climbing and Jack fell silent as he studied the ground beneath him. We were rising above the wall now and I could see that what had appeared a solid impenetrable barrier was, in reality a series of great jagged humps of rock, rising high into the air. They were, indeed quite breath-taking to look at, with their rough and broken faces, their thick white caps, and their long green dresses.

But for all their beauty, I found them a little too large and massive. To me, they were scary still. Looking far below, I could see mists caught between the enormous towers that rose to such heights on all sides. As we passed quite close to the side of one mountain, I realised that what I had mistaken for blades of grass on its huge sides were, in reality, trees, dwarfed by its sheer size.

Quite suddenly, I knew that I was looking back centuries in time. That these mountains were the same as they had been hundreds, even thousands of years ago, and that here was, as Jack had tried to tell me, one place that the war had never touched.

We passed over and around several of the immense and intimidating masses and entered a fairly flat area. It was flanked on all sides by the imposing mountains, but still free of their shadows. I had been feeling like a mere speck in the sky and was enjoying the respite of a little more familiar scenery when I noticed a crevice cut into the ground below.

Though it was almost obscured by the trees which grew so thickly about it, and looked like little more than a black slit, I could still see that it was enormous in size, by far the largest that we had encountered. It was easily wider than Master's entire farm, and it stretched as far as we could see, even from our height.

Jack began circling down toward it in dizzying loops and I closed my eyes, trying not to feel the motion. The plane finally levelled out and I opened them again. We were nearly touching the tops of the trees on the level and as we approached nearer to the crevice, I was astonished to see several brightly-coloured bubbles rising up out of it and above the trees. More and more of them rose until there were dozens floating about in the sky above us.

Jack pushed forward on the framework and pulled back on the lever and the plane began to lower itself until we were just above the crevice. I realised that I had again grasped the sides of my chair as I felt the plane descend. We flew straight for several seconds, and then Jack sent the plane down once more. The great walls seemed to close over us and we were inside.

Everywhere was green. I had never imagined such a sight. There were deep green trees, deep green grasses, even deep green houses, in neat rows. It was like sailing into a deep green pocket.

Jack turned the plane and I saw a green field stretching out before us. We descended further and the field seemed to open up to receive us. The wheels began to bump along and I knew that we were once more on the ground. The speed slackened and finally we were standing still in the middle of the field.

Ross and Mia and I just sat, hardly daring to move, but Jack unhooked his belt and rose. But without his usual vigour. He seemed shaky. Weak.

I moved quickly to help him, pulling his arm over my shoulder and wrapping my other arm around the slight body, trying to take some of his weight. Together, we moved slowly to the back of the plane. Then Jack signalled for Ross to open the door and push the folding stairway once more outside.

"Come," he said, "We have made it." He pushed me behind him and stepped out the door.

I glanced down at the hand that had been supporting Jack and was surprised to see that it was covered in something red. And sticky.

Blood.

Then Jack collapsed.

CHAPTER NINE

I stared, horrified, as Jack's limp body tumbled down the stairs. As quickly as I could, I started down.

But Ross was faster. He simply ignored the stairs all together and leaped from the door to land beside Jack.

He had straightened Jack out on the grass and we both gasped as we saw the large red stain that nearly covered the left side of his white robes. Ross hurried to unbutton them.

"He has been injured," Ross said. "Probably by the guns."

"Guns?"

"A weapon invented by men to kill," Ross said. "I have seen them used on injured horses." He lifted his head and looked at me. "They were firing them at us."

"They?"

"The riders. Back when we stopped."

Suddenly, I understood the popping sounds I had heard. Guns.

"But..." I got no further.

A shadow fell across us. Expecting to see Mia, I looked up.

Several strange males were standing beside us.

I gasped.

Then Jack's eyes opened. "Ah," he said. He took a deep breath and his face puckered. Then he shook his head and began speaking.

Words that I couldn't recognize.

I looked at Ross, but, from the look on his face, he was as confused as I.

But if we couldn't understand Jack, it was obvious that these strange men did. They immediately knelt beside him and pulled back the edges of his uniform.

A long gash was disclosed. An ugly tear in the flesh across Jack's side.

I gasped.

One of the men leaned over Jack and gently poked at the wound. Jack shook his head and said something.

The man nodded.

Jack looked at me. "It's not as bad as it seems, Liss," he said. "The bullet merely grazed me."

"Bullet?"

He sighed. "Another something to explain when we have time." He smiled wanly at Ross and I. "I'm so sorry that I alarmed you by fainting," he said, "I'm actually not feeling too bad. I think it was mostly that I'm tired."

I nodded my head, though I was having a hard time understanding.

Someone had brought a basket and now handed it to one of the men kneeling beside us. He wet a cloth with some liquid from a bottle, then washed Jack's wound, carefully.

Jack winced and I was reminded of the time I had been helped by the healers at Masters. I knew what Jack was feeling.

Very quickly and efficiently, the man cleaned and bandaged. Then he re-buttoned Jack's clothing and helped him to sit up.

Jack looked quite shaky, still, so I moved close to him, prepared to help him once more.

But the healer was quicker than me and he helped Jack instead; sitting down beside him and putting a supporting arm around the aged shoulders.

Jack looked up at me and stretched his mouth.

I watched him carefully for a moment, then took a deep breath of clear, fragrant air and, for the first time, looked around.

A large group of people had approached from the north and was dividing their attention between our aeroplane and us. Like most of the workers I had known, their hair was dark, but beyond that there was very little similarity between us. Here, the hair was of differing lengths - some of the females had even allowed theirs to grow far down their backs.

Their skin, too was different. While it was not as light as mine, neither was it as dark as Ross and Mia's, but rather a shade somewhere between the two. Their height was comparable to ours, but their weight was far above our own. They easily outweighed any of us by half.

But the difference I found most noticeable was the colour of their clothing.

Or I should more accurately say, 'colours'.

Every colour that I had ever seen in Little Artist's palette, and more, was standing before me in the clothing worn by these people. And in every variation imaginable from the darkest, deepest shades through to pale colours that were almost white.

The males wore a sort of half-robe that covered their bodies from waist to knees, and the females had either wrapped yards and yards of cloth around their bodies, or were dressed in a loose, flowing robe similar to that affected by the masters, but without the hood.

I found myself wondering if we were seeing workers or masters, forgetting for the moment that, according to Jack, we were the only workers present.

The entire group watched us closely, without making a sound. I noticed that many of them held onto slender pieces of cord and more of the bright bubbles we had seen in the sky bobbed and danced at the other end of them.

Not knowing what to do, I shrank into the shadow cast by the plane, and waited for some hint from Jack. I glanced up at the plane. Mia's frightened face showed briefly in the doorway, before disappearing back into the plane. Ross had retreated to the plane as well, standing uncertainly at the bottom of the stairs.

With the help of the healer, Jack rose slowly to his feet. He said something to the healer, who stretched his mouth and briefly bent forward at the waist before turning and walking away.

Then Jack turned toward the assembled group and said something in that same strange language, sweeping his arms apart as he did so to indicate Ross, Mia and I.

Instantly the people stretched out their mouths, showing their teeth, and began to speak excitedly, some making a strange clucking noise as they did so. They reached out their hands to grasp his.

Suddenly, someone spoke a single word above the noise and everyone became silent, moving aside to allow the passage of a strange and majestic figure. As it grew closer, I could see that it was a female and as tall a person as I had ever seen. She was completely draped in a huge cape, orange and far brighter than any clothing we had seen here, and she wore a hat, which reached high into the air.

It was not like the shade hats given to the workers at Master's, neither was it like the hoods worn by the masters, but it seemed an impractical mass of flowers, leaves and feathers and could serve no purpose other than to give added height.

The female approached Jack, held out her hand and spoke to him. Again the words were strange.

He responded, grasping her hand briefly with his own.

She showed her teeth to him and turned. Raising her hands high in the air, she clapped them together once and then spread them out before her.

Instantly, everyone began to talk and gesture wildly, many again making the strange clucking sound. A small group sat down where they were and produced small barrels, which they placed before them. Then they began thumping their hands on the leather stretched tightly across one end, producing a regular rhythm.

Others moved away from the main group and began swaying their bodies in time to the beat in a manner that was, at once, strange and familiar. I found myself wanting to join them and move as they did, though I had no idea of why I was thinking this way.

Another group ran off in the direction from which we had come. I could only imagine that they were going back to the houses over which we had flown.

The tall female had disappeared and I stood up and looked through the remaining talking, gesticulating crowd for her. At last I saw her, but was surprised to see that she was much shorter.

She was standing beside Jack, so I made my way toward them.

As I pressed through the crowd, people reached out towards me, touching gentle fingers to my hair and making the strange clucking as they did so. Some even tried to offer the two-armed salute, but those, I managed to elude. A little breathless, I reached Jack's side. He turned at my hesitant touch.

"Ah, here you are," he said, stretching his lips and showing his teeth. He took my hand and turned to the female, again speaking in that strange, rather liquid-sounding speech. She looked at me, also stretching her lips and replied.

Then she reached for the hand that Jack held and gave it a squeeze.

"Liss, this is Ramannah, the Queen of this people," he said.

"Queen?" I repeated rather breathlessly.

"Erm…leader."

I nodded my comprehension.

As the crowd moved away a little, I was able to get a clearer view of this 'Queen'. She had laid aside the voluminous cloak and enormous hat and I realised that she was not much taller than I, though a good deal heavier.

She wore a simple pink robe, much the same style as many of the others. Her hair was black, though it was heavily streaked with grey. Her skin was quite dark and it was smooth and unmarked, except around her eyes where tiny lines had been etched, radiating out from the outer corners.

She again stretched her mouth, disclosing even white teeth, narrowing her eyes as she did so. The lines about her eyes

74

deepened and I guessed that it was this action that had caused them.

I wondered briefly about her change in height until I saw that a strange pair of boots dangled from her other hand. They had a light leather top, shaped much as my own, but with several large pieces cut away, making them a mere framework. The sole of the 'boots' was amazingly thick – several hand breadths thick, and I could see now, that this was what had given Ramannah her height.

As I watched, she handed them to a female standing near who already carried her cloak and hat. Then she sighed and seated herself on the soft grass. She pulled the skirt of her robe up to her knees, crossed her legs and gestured for us to join her.

Jack immediately, and with a heavy sigh, sank down beside her.

I had never seen so much flesh exhibited at one time and it made me very conscious of where my eyes rested. She wore no socks and her feet remained bare. She seemed to prefer it so. As I glanced around, I realised that very few of the people wore shoes. Looking down, I curled my toes in my boots and tried to imagine what the grass would feel like.

I noticed that most of the people had copied her manner and were seating themselves all around us, still talking excitedly.

Ramannah said something to Jack in the strange, liquid speech of hers and Jack replied. They spoke for several minutes, then he turned and deciphered it for me.

"Ramannah just told me that she was very pleased we were able to join in their celebration," he said. At my puzzled look, he clucked deep in his throat. "I told her that we really didn't know about their celebration – that our arrival was purest coincidence. She said they were pleased anyway. She has offered to include us in the festivities."

"Festivities?" I echoed weakly.

"They are celebrating the arrival of spring and the return of life," he said. "You won't understand this at this moment, but I think it was a very apt and appropriate time for us to come." I frowned. He was right. I didn't understand.

He stretched his mouth. "We, too are celebrating our return to life!"

CHAPTER TEN

Suddenly, above the hubbub of the crowd, I heard a noise that was almost frightening. It sounded as if several people were simply opening their mouths and letting their voices come as loudly as they could. I saw everyone near me show his or her teeth and turn towards the sound. I did my best to see past them.

From the direction of the houses came a large group of young-ones, moving at top speed. There were males and females - some tall, able to outdistance the others easily, and some barely able to walk at all and helped by adults. Then I saw several more adults bringing up the rear and they were carrying young-ones so small that if they stood, they would hardly reach my knees. Still others held small bundles snugly wrapped in blankets.

"Ah, the children," Jack said, stretching his mouth. "They must have been sent inside for safety when they heard our plane."

"Children?" Almost without thinking, I stood up and walked over to one of the females carrying a small blanket-wrapped bundle.

I gazed down at it in curiosity. To my surprise, it, too was a young-one, but so tiny that it was hardly bigger than my boots. It was sleeping, eyes tightly shut and mouth moving quietly. I reached out a tentative finger and touched a soft cheek, pulling my hand away as it stirred slightly.

The adult holding it was a female and I looked up at her. She was watching me closely and finally she looked over at Ramannah. Ramannah nodded slightly and the female held the young one up as though she wanted me to take it.

I backed away, shaking my head from side to side negatively. She moved toward me and again held her arms up a little, giving me a clearer view of the tiny form. I stopped, captivated by feelings that I cannot describe. Then I turned and looked at Jack.

He nodded and gestured towards the bundle.

I hesitated a few moments longer, then I carefully studied the way the female held her arms and tried to shape my own into the same configuration. She laid the young-one into the nest I had formed and for the first time in my life, I held another person.

The same warm feeling I had experienced before came over me, but stronger, almost frightening in its intensity. I looked down at the little sleeping face and quite suddenly I knew that this is what a young-one looks like just after it receives life.

That this is what grows inside when one is carrying and what is removed when the time for marking comes.

My feelings intensified even further and I felt as if I would do almost anything to protect this little being. It was as if this young-one and I were connected in some way by invisible cords that were attached deeply within me.

I stood looking down at it and suddenly, inexplicably, I felt water welling up in my eyes again. I blinked several times, trying not to allow the moisture to blur my vision. Then the tiny form began to stir, raising two little fists above its head and arching up and away from my arms.

In alarm, I handed it to the female and stepped back, afraid I had injured it in some way. She simply jogged it gently up and down in her arms for a moment and it settled back into sleep.

I brushed at my eyes with the back of my hand, staring in curiosity at the water I found there, then moved closer for a last look at the young-one. My chest ached as I watched the female suddenly bring the tiny form close to her and press her lips to the soft skin of the curving forehead, and I turned away, going once more to sit beside Jack.

"There is a good reason for what you are experiencing," he said to me, reaching out a hand and clasping my shoulder. "Your feelings will be explained - soon."

Everywhere were the young-ones, talking excitedly to the adults, leaping about to the rhythm of the barrels, climbing around and inside the aeroplane, or simply tumbling together in the soft grasses.

From the time that I had left the growing buildings, I had not been in close proximity with young-ones, and I found their shrill, high-pitched voices brought back memories of my own young days. I felt drawn to them but at the same time almost confused by the cacophony of sound that seemed to accompany them.

Jack was watching my face. I fleetingly wondered if he could see my confused thoughts.

He could. "Perhaps you should begin to understand," he said. "You have questions, Liss?"

"Many," I answered immediately. "Everything has been so confusing and I realise that there is much to learn. But I will start with one question." I looked at him and placed a hand over my chest.

"What am I feeling? Here." I put one hand on my chest.

Jack opened his mouth and put his head back and gave a loud clucking noise. Startled, I moved slightly away from him. He straightened up and turned to me, wiping his hands over his eyes as he did so.

"I'm sorry, Liss," he said. "It was just a funny way of starting out."

"Funny?" I asked.

"Uh…something that makes you feel pleasant inside."

"I have felt things like that," I said, "But that is not the emotion that is confusing me now."

"I know, Liss, I know," he said, calming down. "You are confused by the warm feelings that you are experiencing, right."

"Warm. Yes. I am."

"Those are the normal natural feelings that most humans feel or are supposed to feel. Those are feelings of affection, of love, of caring. They are the feelings that held our world together in the Before Times, and that the Masters have tried to eliminate."

He continued, "Fortunately, they did not eliminate the feelings, merely the names. The people still felt, they just did not know what they were feeling."

I spoke up, "I have experienced these warm feelings as you say, but they are different. I feel something for Meg, but I feel something totally different for…for…someone."

Jack looked at me closely, but said nothing.

I went on, "And just now, I felt the strongest feeling of all, while I was merely holding a tiny young-one. Can you explain this to me?"

"I think it is a topic that will take some time, but I will try to give you some idea," Jack said. He looked around at the people and then back at me.

"In the Before Times, males and females—or men and women, as I prefer that they are called; or more correctly, *a* man and *a* woman would marry or join their lives together. They would live in the same room and they would welcome and raise young-ones. All of them together were what was called a family. They cared deeply for each other, and it was the strongest force in the world. Almost everyone who came from a close family became a productive member of society. They had fewer problems and were better able to cope with life. It is a small part of these deep feelings that you experienced when holding that infant."

"Infant?"

"A very new young-one."

"Oh," I said. I really didn't understand, but I thought he needed to feel successful.

His voice changed subtly. "The war began to alter all of this. As the masters took over, they tore the families apart and thus weakened our country. Individuals had to stand on their own and were easily led and controlled. There is an old saying, 'Divide and Conquer', not coined to describe families, but just as effective in destroying them and, essentially, the fabric upon which we were built."

Jack looked away and was silent for a second. I was surprised to notice water brimming in his tired eyes. Impatiently he scrubbed at them with the back of his hand. Then he turned back to me, finally noticing my obvious confusion. "I'm sorry, Liss. I didn't need to go into that. I am merely trying to give you some idea of the use for your feelings. You will understand more as you study these people."

I looked around at the group and could see males and females - or men and women, as Jack called them - with their arms across each other's shoulders or around each other's waists. I saw young-ones riding on adult shoulders and being cradled gently in adult arms.

I shook my head. It was all most confusing.

"Are you through with questions, already, Liss?" Jack asked as the silence grew longer.

"No, Jack. There is so much more I need to know. It is hard to put it into a question. Why do they touch?"

"Touching is a way of showing the affection I have been telling you about," he said.

"Affection?"

Those warm feelings we were discussing," he said.

I was puzzled.

"How can I explain this…? You know that there are some foods that you like."

"Yes."

"And there are some things that you like."

"Yes."

"Well it is possible to like people also. My analogy isn't really accurate, but it is the closest I can come to explaining it."

"I knew it…I knew it!" I said excitedly. "Often at Master's I wanted to sit next to some of the workers—Meg especially. I felt calm inside when I was near her. And whenever…er…someone else was around, I wanted to be near…that person. Is this what liking someone means?"

He was watching me. Finally, he shrugged. "Yes," he answered, stretching his mouth.

I tipped my head to one side, watching curiously. "What is that you are doing?" I asked him.

He frowned slightly, not understanding my question. "Am I doing something?" he said, stretching his mouth again.

"Yes," I said, pointing to his lips. "There—with your mouth!"

"Oh!" he said, realisation dawning in his face. "That is a smile. I'm smiling!"

"Why do you do it?" I asked.

"That is what you do when you are feeling pleasant—when you are with someone you have warm feelings for, or doing something you enjoy." He stretched his lips—smiled—once more. "It is also the best and easiest way to pretty up your face," he said.

"Pretty up?" I echoed.

He sighed. "Something else we will have to go into," he said.

I touched my lips with my fingers. Then I tried to copy Jack's action, stretching my mouth and showing my teeth. He caught his breath.

"Liss," he said quietly, "You truly are beautiful!"

I looked at him, again failing to understand.

He said nothing but continued to look at me. I went back to practising my smile.

He shook his head and leaned back, staring up into the impossibly blue sky. "Do you think you understand about feelings now?" he asked.

I thought for a moment. I had certain strange and uncomfortable feelings whenever Young Master was about, and I knew that what I felt for him and what I felt for Meg were not the same. I knew, too that the intense emotion I had experienced when I held the tiny young-one was different again. Apparently, I had experienced different kinds and that was normal.

I frowned. Each feeling was too new and wonderful for me to discuss in anything but general terms, and I could not admit any curiosity about the masters to Jack, so further discussion on that subject needed to be cut short.

For the first time in my life, however, my lack of knowledge did not alarm me. I felt that, in time, I would know.

There was another thing that was confusing to me and I felt that it would not be as difficult for Jack to explain. "I do have another question, Jack. What is the strange clucking noise everyone makes?"

"That 'clucking' noise you have noticed usually accompanies a smile and is called laughter, an expression of extreme happiness."

"Smiling. And laughter. I have never experienced these before."

"I know that. You will be seeing a great many things that you have never seen before.

I turned again to look at the people seated about me. The young-ones had found Ramannah, and she had a large group of them clustered about her. Several were not satisfied with squatting on the ground before her and these were sitting on her legs or standing behind her and leaning forward with their arms around her neck.

Occasionally, one would press his or her lips against the elder's smooth cheek. They seemed to love to touch and be close to her and to each other. She was speaking to them. Because of the noise about me, I couldn't hear much of what she said, and couldn't understand what I did hear, but the young-ones were totally absorbed in her words. I saw them look towards me from time to time, and I guessed that Ramannah was telling them about the strange new people in their midst.

"I have one more question," I said, looking over the bright group.

"Ask away," Jack said.

"Why do they wear the colours? They are not dressed in the whites and blues of Masters and Workers."

"A very good question," Jack said, smiling. "And it is for a very good reason." He shifted slightly. "They wear different colours than the masters and workers because they don't recognize the same order here."

I looked at him, not understanding.

"There *are* no masters or workers here."

I thought about that for a moment. "You said something similar to that before, but I thought you meant that everyone here was a Master."

Jack smiled again. "Well, in a sense, everyone is," he said.

"A Master."

"Yes. Because they are free."

"Free?"

"Each person makes their own choices and decisions."

"Where they work?"

"Yes."

"What they wear? And eat?"

"Yes."

"How they live?"

"Most definitely. Free."

CHAPTER ELEVEN

I suddenly realised that I had not seen Ross or Mia for some time, and glanced at the plane. Ross' giant form no longer stood at the steps and I could see into the shadowy interior enough to know that Mia no longer hid there.

I looked through the colourful crowd for a glimpse of blue cloth, or a familiar dark-skinned face, but they didn't appear to be among the people here. Fearing for their safety, I stood up and looked carefully in all directions.

The sun had gone behind the wall of cliffs on the west, but the sky remained luminous with light and the area was still bright. Along the base of the west wall, a large stream of water flowed quietly. Though the day was warm, a mist hung over the strange dark green water, and I wondered what it contained to make it so peculiar a colour and to make it steam in the shadows.

Alongside the eastern bank of the stream, trees sprouted to an immense height and I knew from my earlier discussions with Jack during our flight that their haphazard arrangement indicated they had grown there naturally and had not been brought from some distant spot. They extended as far as the eye could see and coyly screened a clear view of the water.

South of me, I could see only the field that we stood upon. It appeared to extend for miles and resembled a thick green blanket covering a large portion of the land. A little way off, a large herd of cattle grazed quietly and from their shining skin and rounded forms, I knew that they were well fed and healthy. Many had very young calves at their sides and at the sight of them, my mind returned briefly to my ledgers at home and my records of such additions to Master's properties. These people were wealthy indeed.

To the east, I saw the cliffs that we had so recently flown over. They formed a mighty wall behind yet another grove of trees - this one more familiar to me as it was placed with precision in long, even rows.

I stared at them for a few moments. Something about them was strange. At first I took them to be covered in snow – something impossible in this warm weather. Then I realised they were so heavily laden with fragrant blossoms that they were white. This was something familiar to me, though I had never seen such abundance in Master's carefully tended orchard. I knew that in due time, these same blossoms would give way to fruit and that I was looking at another of the major sources of food and prosperity for this people.

Turning, I could see that the field extended north as it did south, covering the land in green. The buildings of the people stood under the shelter of the trees on the west in two long rows, and were almost hidden from view, even from quite close.

As I watched, a number of people came out of the last building on the Southwest corner in the group and proceeded to carry large containers and trays towards the river.

Curious, I glanced down at Jack. "What are those people doing?" I asked.

He craned his neck to see. "Looks like dinner to me, Liss," he said, smiling. He started to rise.

I lent him my meagre strength. Then Jack smiled at me. Then the two of us, Jack leaning slightly on me, walked towards the people with the trays.

As we grew closer, I was relieved to glimpse both Ross and Mia in this group. They looked different somehow, and it wasn't until I was very close that I realised that both of them had changed their clothing and were dressed as the rest of the people, Mia, wrapped in a bright pink cloth, covering her from neck to knees and leaving her arms and shoulders bare, and Ross, in a dark green half-robe similar to those worn by the other…men, which left his broad chest bare. Those familiar faces atop such different clothing were strange, indeed.

As the others, they carried huge trays and I could now see that Jack had been right. The trays were laden with many different kinds of foods.

A young woman, small and slight, with dark hair bound into a knot at the back of her head, came out of the building and signalled for us to come to her. I looked at Jack for confirmation and he nodded. With some misgivings, we went over. As we approached, she smiled at me and pointed at herself. "Rebecca," she said.

"Liss," I answered her, copying her gesture.

"Jack," he did the same.

She nodded and turned and went back inside, again beckoning us.

The building was large and spacious, with a very high ceiling, but only one room. Three of its four walls held several windows and a door, all of which stood open to allow the cooling breezes of the late afternoon into the room. It was built out of some kind of light-coloured wood, which, together with the windows and doors, made it very bright inside.

Several heavy tables stood about the room and were being used for various tasks. Some females (women, I corrected myself) were standing beside one, cutting vegetables into small pieces. At another, two more women were scrubbing potatoes and at a third, huge cuts of meat were being sliced by a man and laid on trays.

Along the fourth wall was an enormous brick structure with several heavy doors. These were hinged on the bottom with a large wooden handle at the top and as we watched, Rebecca took yet another tray from a pile on a table and walked over to one.

She placed her tray on a small table, which stood beneath the door, then she grasped the handle and pulled back, letting out a blast of hot air and revealing a large piece of meat which was cooking right inside the structure.

I realised that the brick structure was an oven, but much larger than any I had seen before.

Taking a long hook from the wall, Rebecca reached into the space and pulled on an arm of metal. It swung out and I realised that it had been thrust right through the center of the huge piece of meat. The smell was wonderful and I suddenly felt faint, realising again that my body needed nourishment.

I could only imagine how Jack was feeling, in his weakened condition.

Rebecca hung the large hook back on the wall and grasped two long forks from the tray. Then in one motion, she deftly pulled the meat off the metal arm and placed it on her tray. Bending slightly under the weight, she carried the tray over to the man who was slicing meats. Then, wiping her hands on a cloth, she turned to me. "Come," she said, gesturing for us to follow her.

Surprised at hearing a familiar word from her, I hesitated.

Jack smiled. "It's okay, Liss," he said.

"Come," she said again. We followed.

Rebecca led us out another of the doors and we were almost immediately inside yet another building. It was different from the last, though it was built of the same materials and had the same high ceiling. This building contained several rooms, leading off one central corridor.

Looking down the hallway in which we stood, I could see through another doorway and into a third building. The structures here had been assembled very close together and the doors were all ajar, so it seemed as though one could walk the entire length of the settlement almost without stepping outside.

Rebecca moved purposefully down the hallway and we continued to follow her, glancing quickly into each open doorway as we passed. The first room contained only huge rolls of brightly-coloured cloth. There were shelves lining the walls and reaching to the ceiling and all of them were piled high.

In the second room, several men and women were sitting, talking together and working with pieces of cloth. I guessed that they were fashioning new robes for the people.

Rebecca paused in that doorway and said something in her own language. The people looked up and smiled, then immediately set down whatever they had been working on and got to their feet.

Rebecca smiled and continued down the hall.

"Call to dinner," Jack whispered to me.

I nodded.

It was as we paused before the doorway leading to the third room that I felt grateful that I had had the care of Master's records and transactions. When Master had decided that we would make our own cloth, he had studied many different types of equipment. After he had made his decisions and completed his orders, all his notes and several pictures were given into my keeping. I had examined these carefully.

For this reason, I could easily identify the bundles of raw wool and cotton, the spinning wheels, and towards the back of the room, the looms standing in a circle and being put to use by several chattering adults. I could hear the thump as these large machines were manipulated by the workers and for a moment, the familiar sound transferred me back to Master's offices with Mia and her crew working in the building nearby.

Once more, Rebecca spoke to these people and they happily got to their feet and hurried towards the door. Rebecca waited until they had all left the room, then gestured for us to follow her and slipped through the doorway.

Rebecca crossed the room and opened one of several doors. A small closet was revealed. Then she opened a second door beside it, revealing another. She then turned away and walked over to a set of shelves lining the wall behind the bundles of wool.

Reaching up, she plucked down several neatly folded piles of material and brought them over, holding them up for both of us to see and indicating that we should go into the closets.

Jack smiled at her and said something in her language.

She nodded and replied.

"She wants us to change our clothes," he said. He glanced down at his blood-stained robes. "I think it would be a very good idea."

"Will you be all right?" I asked him.

"I'm fine, Liss," he said. "Just a bit weak." He smiled. "Nothing some clean clothes, a good meal, and a week's rest won't cure!"

I clutched the bundle Rebecca had given me and turned slowly, poking my head timidly through the doorway.

There was no ceiling on the little room. It was simply a box built of wood, standing against the inside wall of the building. Its topless state caused it to be quite light inside and I finally overcame my hesitation and stepped inside, pulling the door shut behind me.

Inside, I had no difficulty in seeing what Rebecca had handed me. Several simple, ankle length robes in various colours, with long sleeves and a dozen buttons closing the front. There was also a length of bright blue cloth, obviously meant to be wrapped around my body and tucked within itself to fasten.

I chose one of the robes. A bright orange.

If I were staying for any length of time in the closet, I could rely on the cloth. But I feared that I would soon be leaving the private confines of the little room and would then risk losing the simple cloth and finding myself in the center of the settlement clothed in less than a conventional manner.

I had just finished removing my own uniform and was fastening the robe about me when a single knock on the door startled me. I reached out, swung it open, and was relieved to see Rebecca's face.

She showed her teeth in a wide smile as she looked at my new garment. Then she brushed past me and gathered up my blue clothing and the rest of the robes.

I stepped out of the little room and glanced around. Jack still hadn't emerged. I moved over to the second door and tapped on the wood.

"Almost there!" Jack said.

"Are you well?" I asked.

"Good as I'll ever be," Jack said. He caught his breath and groaned slightly.

"What is it? What's the matter?" I called out.

"Nothing, Liss," he said. "Just trying to get my left arm into the sleeve."

"Is it hurting your wound?"

"A bit."

The door swung open. "What do you think?" he asked.

Jack was now dressed in a robe of rich brown. Earth brown.

I stretched my mouth in a smile. "You look...different," I managed finally.

He clucked...laughed. "Thanks, Liss, I'll try to not let your compliments go to my head!"

I stared at him uncomprehendingly. "Compliments?"

He laughed again. "It's called sarcasm, Liss," he said. Then he sighed. "Something else I will need to teach you later." He handed his soiled white robe and blood-stained under garments to Rebecca and said something to her in her own language.

She laughed.

I took Jack's arm once more and the two of us, looking very different from when we had entered, followed Rebecca back into the long hallway and we retraced our steps into the large cooking building.

From there, she led us out of the western door and to a small building further under the trees. Looking inside, I was relieved to notice that it was a toilet building and I looked gratefully at Rebecca and disappeared inside.

Then we allowed Jack his turn, and the three of us returned once more to the cooking building. This time, Rebecca moved over to one of the tables, which held the filled platters and handed one of them to me. Then she picked up a second one and walked ahead of us and out the door through which we had entered only a few minutes before.

We made our way slowly towards the river, following a broad, well-trodden path through the trees. I looked down at the tray I was carrying and felt my body grow weak once more at the sight and smell of the roasted meats.

I glanced at Jack. He, too, was eyeing the tray with apparent interest.

A large group, probably the whole settlement, had gathered under the huge trees at the edge of the gently flowing water. They had spread out cloths the same colour as the grass beneath them and had laid out the trays piled high with food of every description.

At Master's the food had been nourishing and plentiful, but here my mind swam at the seemingly endless supply of meats, vegetables, breads, fruits, and cheeses, as well as many platters of things that I simply could not put a name to.

Rebecca set her tray and then mine among those already laid out. As I stood there, Ramannah emerged from the crowd and took a place on one side of the cloth about halfway from either end.

As if they had been given a command, everyone else began to scramble for a place, smiling, talking and laughing loudly.

Ramannah waved to Jack and he moved slowly towards her, taking a seat beside her. I smiled at him. Now that he was dressed in the flowing, colourful robes of these people, he could easily be one of them. His eyes moved over the crowd until they found me. He smiled into my eyes, gesturing for me to join him.

I made my way around the food and across to the other side, finally finding a place to sit between Jack and another man.

Then as everybody became settled, Ramannah slapped her hands together. Instantly, silence fell across the group. Ramannah said something to the huge man beside me and he rose to his feet. Then he bent his head down and closed his eyes.

I glanced straight ahead and caught the puzzled eyes of Ross and Mia, who were seated across from me. They too, were wondering what was happening. I turned to look at Jack and saw that he had bent his head and was waiting quietly and as I looked past him, I could see that everyone was following his manner, with the exception of some of the smaller young-ones who were looking at the piles of food.

Copying Jack, I grasped my hands tightly in my lap and bowed my head, though I kept my eyes open to see what would happen.

Suddenly the man began to speak and for a long time, his liquid speech rose and fell on the breeze. Then he said one last word, which everyone repeated after him, sat down, and the meal began.

Everyone was reaching for the food. Adults handed choice bits to young-ones. I watched as a young woman carefully chewed up a small piece of meat and placed it gently between the lips of a tiny young-one seated on the lap of a man beside her. The tiny one chewed busily on the meat. When it finished and swallowed, it smiled and I saw that it only had four white teeth with which to eat.

Jack had started to make his meal, I noticed, so I again copied his manner. I reached for familiar things first, sliced potatoes and turnips and carrots. My hunger was ruling me by this time and I ate faster and faster in an effort to subdue it. I tried various pieces of meat and found them all delicious. I sampled strange-looking breads covered with a dark-brown coating and discovered a taste sweeter than honey itself.

I tried thick slices of more familiar-looking bread and more of the vegetables, and finally, my hunger gone, reached for the fruit with which to end my meal.

As I licked my fingers and glanced around, I noticed that most of the people were relaxing or simply picking at bits of food as they spoke to the person next to them. The meal seemed to be over. I was amazed at how much had been consumed.

Jack, too, had finished eating and had lain back in the soft grass. He was gazing up through the tree branches over him and into the sky, a soft, sleepy smile on his face.

Someone started to speak, but not in any manner to which I was accustomed. He allowed his words to drag out, to run into each other, and his voice became higher and lower as he willed. The effect was relaxing and very pleasant to the ear. Soon everyone had joined in, saying the words together and making their voices blend. For no reason, I found myself thinking of the young-ones that I had grown with in the growing buildings at Master's. I turned to Jack, my mouth already opened on a question.

His eyes were closed. For a moment, I felt fear. Then I saw the narrow chest rise with a breath and realized that he was simply asleep.

I looked down at him and felt my chest swell strangely. This man had risked so much for me. Suddenly, I felt as though I would do anything for him. He needed a place to take his rest. I looked around, hoping that I could alert someone to this.

But Ramannah had already seen his plight and was signalling for two of the strong young men to carry him toward the buildings.

I stood, ready to follow, but Ramannah waved me back.

As I watched the young men bear him away, I remembered that Jack was old, perhaps too old to have even attempted what he had accomplished in this past 24 hours. As he and his two escorts move out of sight, I hoped that he would not be ill and I knew I had discovered that I "cared", and that to care meant to worry about someone else even more than you did about yourself. I caught my breath.

It was so simple.

The light was fading now over the area and everyone began to separate. Rebecca stood nearby and directed the collection of the food and trays, and many began walking along the same path that we had followed to reach this peaceful spot.

Mia and Ross came over to me and we stood in some confusion, not sure where we were to go from here. Ramannah approached and I was relieved to see Rebecca join her, a young man at her side.

"You come," Ramannah said, pointing to Mia and I and then to Rebecca. Then she pointed to Ross. "You come," she said again, this time patting the shoulder of the man. "Stephen," she said.

Stephen moved off along the trail and Ross fell into step beside him. Mia and I followed Rebecca and all of us trailed up towards the buildings. I looked back. Ramannah remained where she was, watching us. As we reached the clearing between two long rows of buildings, Stephen and Ross moved off toward the structures on the East Side. The rest of us continued along those on the west.

Rebecca passed the two large buildings that I had visited earlier, and several smaller ones, whose windows were already agleam with light. I caught the sound of quiet voices and soft laughter as we passed, as well as the occasional sleepy murmur of a young-one's voice.

Finally, she stopped in front of a small building much like the others except for the darkened windows. She paused only for a moment, however, before she started around the building and beckoned to us. We followed and soon found her standing by yet another small building, not unlike the toilet building I had seen earlier.

I went inside and Mia followed, encouraged by Rebecca's presence close behind her. It was very dim inside, but I could make out several cubicles and I was greatly relieved to notice that the main room also contained a huge bathtub and four buckets.

Mia and I each chose a cubicle, and when we had finished, and stepped back outside, Rebecca was just returning with two buckets filled to the brim. She emptied them into the tub and turned to go back outside, carrying the now-empty buckets with her. She stopped and jerked her head towards the outside and held up the buckets. Each of us grabbed one of the two remaining and followed her. She walked towards the river flowing quietly several yards away from the tiny building.

When she reached the bank, she set one of the buckets down on the sand and pushed the other into the quiet water. Lifting it, she set it down and repeated the process with the other. Then she stood back and indicated that we should fill ours as well. We did so. Then we fell into step behind her. I shifted my load from one hand to the other, slopping the water as I did so. I gasped, expecting to feel a shock of cold water on my legs and feet. But I received a different surprise. The water was comfortably warm. I stopped and thrust my hand into it. It was the perfect temperature for bathing. I turned to look back at the river. What sort of place was this?

Mia had heard me gasp and had turned in time to watch me make my discoveries. Now she, too tested her bucket of water. I saw the surprise in her eyes as she withdrew her hand. Rebecca was watching us also, and I saw her smile briefly before she turned once more.

She led us back to the toilet building, but halted us on the step, set down her buckets, and went in alone. We heard her moving around inside, then saw the flicker of a match. The room was soon lit by a soft glow and she returned to the door, picked up her buckets and beckoned to us. Mia and I stepped inside. Rebecca was just emptying one bucket into the tub and she motioned for us to do the same. I was suddenly struck by the fact that we had accomplished all of this without a single word being spoken between us. It was almost like being back at the Master's again.

Rebecca opened the doors of a large cupboard which stood in the shadows beside the cubicles and laid out two towels and some soap for us. Then she smiled and left us.

Mia and I looked at each other for a moment. "You go first," I said to her and turning, I went outside and sat down on the front step. It was a very short time later that Mia came outside, fully dressed and rubbing her hair with her towel.

"I have finished, Liss," she said quietly. I rose to my feet and she took my place on the planks.

I was very tired, so I only gave myself cursory washing, and it was barely five minutes later that I joined her, my hair still wet and tousled from a vigorous rubbing with my own towel.

Rebecca appeared out of nowhere and again motioned for us to follow her. She led the way back to the tiny cabin standing just in front of the toilet building and opened the door for us. We looked into the softly lighted interior.

There was only one room, but there were two pallets against the north and south walls, each beneath a window. They were strange, for they did not rest on the floor but stood on four legs, leaving a space of several inches beneath them. A long curtain covered the rest of the north wall and Rebecca pulled it back to disclose two sets of shelves and a long iron bar which stretched between them at a height a little above my own. Our own clothing and necessities had been placed neatly on the shelves and several different-coloured robes were hanging from strange wire frames along the bar.

Rebecca indicated the left-hand shelves and pointed to me. Then she gestured towards the right and pointed towards Mia.

We each had our own space, though it was obvious that we would share the same room. We nodded, and Rebecca smiled and patted each of us on the shoulder, then left, closing the door softly behind her.

Mia and I looked at each other and then began to investigate our new quarters.

As in all the other buildings here, the ceiling was high and I suspected that it had been so designed to keep the room cool during the summer months. Everywhere was the light-coloured wood that I had noticed earlier, and as I turned around, I realised that there was another large window beside the door in the east wall. Beneath it stood a washstand and as I walked closer, I discovered two buckets – one under the drain spout and another obviously full of clean water. I turned back to survey the rest of the room.

The west wall, directly opposite the door was almost covered by a stone structure, not unlike the one in the cooking building, except that this one was considerably smaller and had no doors in the opening at the bottom. By the soot streaking the back and sides of the opening, I knew that it must be for heating our little room, and like the great structure in the cooking buildings, held a fire.

Two long, narrow windows were set into the wall at either end of the structure and I walked over to one and tried to peer out. I caught my breath in surprise and alarm as I glimpsed another person looking in at me, someone with hair the exact shade of my own.

I jumped back and Mia rushed to my side. As she stopped beside me, I was even more surprised to see someone who looked exactly like her join the woman who had so startled me.

Creases appeared in Mia's brow and she lifted her hand towards the window. The woman who so resembled her did the same, and it was then I realised that this was not a window at all, but a sheet of glass that had the ability to reflect everything placed in front of it. It was ourselves that we were looking at. I turned again to the red-haired woman and knew that for the first time in my life, I was seeing myself.

"Mia, it's me," I said, reaching out a hand to touch the cool glass. "This is what I look like, isn't it."

"Yes," she answered, "and this is what I look like?"

"Yes," I replied. The discovery was almost more than we could handle on top the surprises and changes that we had witnessed in the last twenty-four hours and all we could do was stand and stare at ourselves.

I discovered that my eyebrows were the same colour as my hair, and were fine and straight, looking almost like bird's wings. My nose was small, something that I had already concluded from what I could see of it, even without the magic glass, but my mouth was wide, and my teeth when I pulled my lips back were white and even.

My eyes were green, almost the colour of the first new grass in the spring and my eyelashes were very dark and thick and shielded my eyes rather effectively if I chose to lower my lids slightly. My skin was smooth and unlined. My face looked small, smaller than I would have expected and my hair framed it neatly.

Something stirred at the back of my mind, a memory of another face, a face very much like my own—glimpsed at another time. But as quickly as the thought came, it slipped and was gone. I was left with only a vague, uneasy feeling of familiarity.

I tilted my head this way and that to study everything— how the hairs grew, the little discoloured imperfections or dots that traced a path across my nose. I even pulled my lips back and tried to smile, something I discovered to be surprisingly easy.

I glanced at Mia and saw that she was just as absorbed in studying herself and the two of us began to turn about slowly in an effort to see the back also. This was harder, but as we did so, I noticed another tiny imperfection at the back of my neck and I moved closer to the glass and twisted to get a better view.

It was a scar in the shape of a "W" that marked the skin just above the line of my pink robes, a "W" that would be invisible if I had been wearing my regular uniform with its high neck. Mia noticed it at the same time as I did, and slowly turned her back towards the glass in an effort to see the back of her neck. She had a similar scar, though it was much more noticeable with her dark skin and we looked at each other, our eyes wide as we tried to decide what this could mean.

I shook my head and moved away, feeling suddenly, unutterably weary and sat on the bed furthest from the door. Mia also turned away and walked over to the shelves, pulling back the curtain and reaching into her space for a neatly folded bundle. She shook out the folds and I recognised a sleeping garment similar to my own. She turned to look at me and dropped her gaze as she caught my eye. Then I rose and moved toward the shelves and she turned her back and began to remove the cloth, which was wound around her body. I caught a brief glimpse of thick white undergarments before she pulled her sleepwear over her head and smoothed it down over her body. Then I found my own night clothing and did the same, catching her eye briefly as I did so.

We were not used to sharing our quarters with anyone and felt awkward in going through those simple routines that had been ours alone for so long.

I searched in the cupboard until I found the brush I used to clean my teeth and my hairbrush. Then I used the cup to dip some water from the convenient bucket and proceeded to scrub my teeth. The water was tepid and tasted peculiar and I finished rather hurriedly, throwing my dirty water out the front door.

Within a few minutes, we were both ready for the rest we so badly needed.
Mia turned down the lantern and blew it out and we scrambled into our beds. For a long time, I lay awake, listening to the unfamiliar sound of another person breathing quietly in my room.

Finally, the stresses and excitements of the day overcame me and I sank into slumber.

CHAPTER TWELVE

The following few days seemed to melt into each other and create one continual learning experience. We spent our time with the people. With Jack's constant help, we began to learn of their ways. So much of what we were taught was so basic to the makeup of a free human being that it is difficult now, looking back, to actually pinpoint where and when we learned it. For the first time since we were given life, we were encouraged to think, to find out about things which had only vaguely bothered us before. But whether we were actually taught many of these things, or just subconsciously observed and incorporated them, I cannot tell anymore.

Many of these new experiences were of the simplest sort. We learned to give the two-armed salute or 'hug' as Jack called it, without any misgivings. The people here were given to much contact with each other and hugging was very common as well as warm handclasps and hearty slaps on the back. Smiling and laughter were perhaps as common, and we learned both, though the latter was a little harder and more unusual.

During this period of adjustment, small things were very noticeable to us. I became used to the sight of my face in the 'mirror' each morning upon awakening, and I was often amused at the state of my hair.

The females here had smooth, beautiful hair but mine, though I combed it thoroughly, would not lay straight and always caused a good deal of laughter whenever I appeared.

Finally, Rebecca showed me how to use liberal amounts of water to tame the thick strands and I was able to leave my hut with the confidence that my hair was not pointing in every direction at once. Oddly enough, it was at such times that my thoughts would turn, unwillingly, to Young Master and I would wonder what he must have thought of me.

On the first morning, Mia and I slept until just after sunrise. The settlement was awakening and we could hear the sounds of talking and laughter as well as the shrill cries of the young-ones or 'children'. I opened my eyes and for a few minutes could not remember where I was.

For a moment, I was frightened.

But memory soon returned and I turned my head to see Mia looking at me. We nodded to each other and slid out of bed. As the night before, we again tried to dress and go about our various morning routines without looking at each other. It was difficult, but it was also the only way we could cope with the unusual presence of another person. Soon we were both ready and we opened the door.

People were milling about, talking and laughing together and young-ones ran everywhere. Rebecca stood nearby, talking with a group of other females or 'young women' and when she saw us, she came over, smiling broadly and raising her arms to give us a hug. This time I did not avoid her touch and was surprised how pleasant the brief contact was. Rebecca waited outside while we went around our small structure to the toilet building, then rejoined us in front of our room once more and led us to the large cooking building.

Everyone was making his or her way towards the same place, and soon, we were enveloped by the delicious smell of the morning meal cooking. We were each handed a plate filled with food and then we followed the people back outside to the center of the settlement, where the soft grass was clipped short. There, everyone simply sat on the ground and made their meal. Again, adults and young-ones sat together with the little ones being aided by the elders.

I realised that I was hungry, and I looked down at my plate. It was laden with many foods, and I recognised a few. Several pieces of fruit were piled on one side, and an odd-looking egg covered a slice of cooked meat. There was also a stack of thin, golden cakes, dripping with some sort of liquid. They certainly looked different, but I tasted them and found them delicious. I attacked my plate and after we had sat there for a few minutes, first Ross, then, to my relief, Jack, joined Mia and me.

Jack was smiling broadly as he looked down at the three of us. "So, how is life as a free person?" he asked. He lowered himself down beside me.

We all looked at him, not knowing how to answer.

Finally, I spoke up, "I can only speak for myself and I hardly know yet," I said. "So far, my thoughts are mainly in confusion."

"For the first time, I feel quiet inside," Mia said shyly, "I do not understand much of what is going on, but I feel able to wait until it is explained to me. I am not afraid."

Jack smiled at her. The he looked at Ross. "What are you thinking, Ross?" he asked.

Ross answered slowly. "It is not easy to put my thoughts into words," he said. "It is difficult to acknowledge them now that it is permissible. It will take me some time to get rid of my confusion enough to even think of a sensible question."

"I am here," Jack said, "for all of you. Please don't hesitate to ask if there is anything troubling you."

"I have a question," I said. "Mia and I noticed a strange mark on our necks last night. What are they?"

A shadow seemed to cross Jack's face. He sighed deeply. "An unfortunate and eternal reminder of the life we are leaving behind," he said at last.

The three of us were silent, waiting for him to continue.

"Yes?" I said, finally.

"You will find that Ross and I have the same mark," he said. "It is the mark of a worker."

"Oh. Something we are all born with." I stated.

"No! You weren't born with it!" Jack said, his voice loud and sharp. He took a deep breath. "It was done to you as an infant."

"Done to me?" This time it was Ross who spoke.

"Yes. Each of you, when you were born, or when you became a worker, as in my case, were branded as such."

"Branded?"

"A hot iron pressed against your skin, burning and marking it forever."

We were silent for a moment, thinking about his words.

"You mean that I have a mark . . ." Ross began.

"It looks like a 'W'," I said.

". . . burned into my skin?"

Jack sighed again. "Yes, Ross," he said, "forever marking you as a worker in the old order."

I reached my fingers to the back of my neck and ran them across the puckered skin that I had felt my entire life, but only understood now. I could see Mia, and finally, Ross, do the same thing.

"Branded," Ross said.

"But a worker no more," Jack said softly.

Ross stared at the small, frail man and dropped his hand. "Yes," he said, lifting his head. "A worker no more."

Mia and I both copied him. I folded my hands together in my lap.

For several seconds, we sat there, silent.

Then Mia spoke up. "What were all the brightly-coloured bubbles that people were carrying and that we saw floating above here yesterday?"

Jack smiled again and turned to me. "We interrupted a celebration," he said. "Something to do with the springtime, and their hopes for a good season. The return to life." He looked at me intently.

I nodded. All of this, he had explained briefly yesterday.

"But the bubbles?" I persisted.

"These people have long used bags filled with warm air for all sorts of purposes. The bubbles you saw yesterday were some of these bags, sent into the air to delight the children and to show the happiness felt by the whole village. I suspect that it is one of their most joyous customs. We happened to appear just as the bubbles, or 'balloons' were set free."

"Set free," I echoed.

Jack kept watching me. "It has a nice sound, doesn't it?" he asked quietly.

CHAPTER THIRTEEN

For the first few days, I was content to study the people and learn from their ways, but in exploring the settlement one day, I discovered something which Jack called a library, and in so doing, I also discovered a way of learning more than I ever dreamed was possible.

The library was a small building set among the sleeping quarters and was literally *filled* with books of every description. Many of them were written in a language foreign to my own, but one section was devoted to books written in 'English' as Jack called it.

These, I could read.

There were huge volumes which dwarfed my own ledgers back at Master's as well as tiny leather-bound books with pages so whisper-thin that one hardly dared to turn them, and printing so tiny that reading was only possible in strong light, and for short periods of time.

I found books about everything, one of the most notable being human anatomy and reproduction (a much neglected subject at Master's). I discovered, to my shock, just what it was that Master, and indeed, all Masters, had been doing to us, their workers. That, put quite simply, we were being used as slaves and breeding stock.

When I voiced my discoveries to Jack, he simply nodded sadly.

"I wish that you never had to know, Liss," he said. "That is truly something I wish I could have saved you from."

"But you did, Jack," I told him, softly.

He half-smiled. "One starfish," he said.

I looked at him, puzzled.

He sighed. "There is a very old story about a man, who was walking down a beach…"

"I read about beaches," I said. "Strips of land at the edge of large bodies of water."

Jack nodded. "Beautiful places," he said. "But places of death, when the creatures that live in the water are thrown up onto the land."

I had read about them, too. I nodded.

He went on, "The story speaks of a man walking down the beach, where hundreds of starfish lie dying on the sand. He picks one up and throws it back into the water. Another man with him tells him that his actions are futile. That he can never hope to save all of the starfish. That he really isn't making any difference."

Jack smiled slightly. "The man responds by picking up another starfish and throwing it into the water. Then he straightens and looks at his companion. 'It made a difference to *that* starfish,' he says."

I thought about his story for a moment. Then I nodded. "So even though you couldn't save all of the workers, you could save a few."

Jack's smile widened. "Exactly, Liss," he said, squeezing my shoulder.

I thought about that for a moment. Then I turned back to Jack. "What made you choose me?" I asked. "And Ross and Mia?"

He smiled, slightly. "Your story, I'm not quite ready to tell…" He held up a hand as I took a breath and opened my mouth to speak. "It will be told, Liss," he said. "When I am ready."

I closed my mouth.

"But Ross and Mia's story is quite simple," he went on. "I chose them because I could see, as could every master in the vicinity, that they cared deeply for each other."

"I, too saw it," I said. "Though I didn't understand what I was seeing."

"And neither did they," Jack said. "I used to watch them in the early mornings when we were waiting for our daily escort.

They could look at no one or nothing else but each other." He shook his head. "I simply couldn't leave them to be discovered by the masters and separated or sold." His voice lowered. "Or worse."

I stared at him. What could be worse than being sold?

He sighed. "The masters were very cruel, Liss," he said. "If anything threatened their tight little world, it was dealt with, decisively and permanently. If a mere worker wasn't performing to standard, he or she was punished or sold, or very…pointedly…stopped."

I remembered the woman in the Master's garden. And Rodney. Both had been stopped. I nodded.   "I could hate the Masters," I said.

"Don't do it, Liss," Jack said. "Hate doesn't accomplish anything," Jack said. "All it does is create more hate."

I thought about his words for several days.

Then, one evening, Jack and I were sitting on the front step of my hut, watching the sun dip below the western cliffs. A group of small boys were playing a game a short distance away. There was a scramble for one of the playing pieces, a hard, wooden ball.

One of the boys, the smallest and quickest, managed to grab it. Then he held the ball aloft in triumph, leaping happily around and through the rest of the players.

Another boy, one of the largest, suddenly stuck out a foot. The smaller boy tripped over it, upending painfully into the dust of their playing area. As he fell, his grip on the ball was lost.

There was another scramble and the larger boy, the one who had been the instigator, emerged triumphant.

His march to the edge of the field was cut short by yet another boy, who charged at him and wrapped both arms around his legs. The victor went down in a heap. Then the other boy sat on his chest and started hitting him—chanting some words with every blow.

Jack started to get to his feet, but settled back as other adults came running. He shook his head. "The boy on top is telling the other boy not to hit his brother!"

The adults pulled the two boys apart and tried to calm everyone down.

Finally, order was restored. When the small boy was questioned, he told them all something.

"He's telling them that someone tripped him."

"As we saw," Liss said.

Jack nodded.

The boy who had started everything was questioned next. Tears were streaming down his cheeks as he spoke.

"Good boy, Dave," Jack said. He looked at Liss and indicated the boy. "He's admitting to the prank."

Finally, the third boy was brought forward. He, too, was crying. He said something, his tears making tracks down his dusty cheeks.

"Ben is saying that the other boy hurt his little brother," Jack said.

One of the men said something.

"He wonders if Ben wanted to hurt Dave."

Ben ducked his head, his eyes on the dirt as his feet. He nodded.

The man said something.

As Ben sat silently, Jack leaned toward Liss. "The man wants to know what Ben got from his anger. And if what he did made his brother feel any better."

Ben lifted his head and looked at Brett, who by now, was also crying.

He shook his head.

The man spoke again.

"He's saying that all that was accomplished was hurting yet another person."

Ben was sobbing now. He said something to the man.

110

Jack smiled. "He's saying he's really sorry. And that he was so angry, he thought he hated Dave. His best friend."

"Dave. The one who stole the ball?" Liss asked.

Jack nodded.

The man was talking to Ben again. He finally put an arm around the boy's shaking shoulders and hugged him.

"He told him that anger and hatred don't solve anything. That, at most, they only make matters worse."

Ben scrubbed at his eyes and looked at the other two boys. Then he nodded, got to his feet and approached Dave.

He said something to the boy and then held out his right hand.

Dave took the proffered hand and shook it slightly. He nodded and said something.

"He's telling Ben it's all right. That he, Dave, started it with his silly prank."

Brett moved between the other two, looked up at them through teary eyes and spoke.

Jack smiled. "Brett wants to know if they are all friends again."

The other two grinned through their own tears.

Both Ben and Dave nodded, their eyes on each other.

The boys moved off towards the main square.

"Pity that all disagreements can't be fixed that easily, isn't it?" Jack said.

"Easily?" I asked.

"Well, a few tears later and they are all friends again."

"I guess," my eyes on the boys as they moved away.

Jack rubbed his forehead. "The wars that were fought here in our world—even this last devastating one—started just as simply," he said. "One person hurt by another. But, instead of talking things out peaceably, the hurt party retaliated…"

"I know. I read all about it in the library," I said, hurriedly. I knew talking about the wars made Jack sad.

Jack nodded. "It's simple mathematics, Liss," he said.

I frowned at him.

"It really is. One person gets hurt. Then they retaliate. Then two people are hurt. That's twice as many."

I took a deep breath and nodded. "I see what you mean," I said.

"Simple mathematics. With each attempt to 'even the score', more people get injured. If it had stopped at the beginning, just one would have been. And that is where it should have stopped."

"Think of all the lives lost or destroyed by simple mathematics," I told him.

"Exactly," he agreed.

Not all of my discoveries were as notable. Most of the books were simply books of facts, some told through pictures, some through story.

I saw beasts and wildlife that were almost impossible to imagine, so different were they from anything I had ever seen. There were giraffes, with necks that stretched far up into the sky and elephants with noses that touched the ground.

There were books which described our world in detail. I had imagined that the land on which we lived, covered all that was inhabitable, but I soon discovered that we lived on only a small part of an enormous, round, planet. A place so big that travel in an attempt to circle it would have taken months, even with Jack's plane.

I read about the old days, even before the Before Times— of Kings and rulers in many different countries, with unpronounceable names like Tanganyika and Czechoslovakia. Of customs and wars and centuries of changes and inventions.

I even stumbled upon a book on farming and discovered a machine very similar to that which had so intrigued me in the museum on the night of our escape. It was called a tractor and had been designed to do all the heavy work now performed by the horses. I discovered that different models could pull as much weight as hundreds, even thousands of horses, and in half the time.

Truly, the Before Times had been remarkable.

It did not take me long to discover that the books I had grown to adulthood with had been painfully dissected, with almost every subject censored in some way. We had glimpsed life as the masters would have us see it, and as I looked at the wealth of information available to me now, I realised just how pitifully narrow my education had been.

Following my discovery of the library, I spent many blissful hours ignoring the people in the settlement and exploring the world through those books, soaking in such unheard-of subjects as politics, social science, biology, communications, and I would have continued on in the same manner, but for the accidental removal of a different volume as I reached up into a shelf high above me. With the opening of its covers, another age greeted me. The book was a plain, thick one, unremarkable, as books go, with a dusty blue cover containing some faded, indecipherable gold lettering. But with the turning of a few stiff, yellowed pages, I was in the last days of the Before Times and the horror and injustice of that period burst upon me both suddenly and completely. I read on, ignoring hunger pangs, oblivious to anything about me, hardly daring to move.

The light faded and the print and pictures became more and more difficult to see, I looked up and was surprised to find that the day was nearly done. I had been reading for hours and had missed at least one meal. It was nearly time for the evening's rest. But I knew there was something I had to do before I could settle for the night. I closed the book and, carrying it, left to search for Jack.

I found him relaxing beside a fire, which had been lit in a pit near the buildings, watching it throw light and sparks high into the night air. He was alone and turned as I approached. I saw his glance take in the book that I carried under my arm.

"We were worried about where you had gotten to, Liss," he said. "Ramannah had just called out a group to start a search when Mia ran up and told us you were in the library, totally absorbed in some book. Ramannah decided to let you remain until you had had your fill of knowledge for the day."

His eyes met mine, "The time has come for some answers, Liss." It was not a question, it was a statement. He knew what it was that I carried and he knew what I had come to him for.

I studied him closely. He had recovered from his piloting ordeal and looked rested and refreshed, but now, I was looking at him as someone that I had never seen before. He was one of the few people who had lived through both times. He was one of those who could still feel and then understand those feelings and yet had survived in the New Age. I laid the book down on the grass between us and opened it to the first page.

"An account of the history of the World from the years 2025 to 2049," I read. "There are facts here," I said, looking at Jack, "but now I need you to fill in the rest."

He was silent for several minutes. "I hardly know where to start," he said, finally. "Where do you begin to tell the story of the end of life as it has been lived for generations?"

"Perhaps you could start with a little background," I said, trying to be helpful. "What was it like before any trouble began?"

He sat up and leaned his forearms on his knees as he stared into the fire. "It was, needless to say, quite different from anything you have experienced," he began. "There had been hundreds, even thousands of different peoples living around the world, but they had been able to rule themselves in their own little countries— choose their own leaders and have a strong voice in what those leaders did," he said. "Everything had seemed peaceful and serene—adults living in harmony with other adults and with children. I touched on that briefly the other day, remember?

I nodded.

"These children—or young-ones to you—had been brought to life through the wishes, and needs, of the adults. The adults, in turn, cared for their children, working where they chose and using money earned to support themselves and their families."

"You mentioned that before, and I have read that they actually lived together in the same building. I have been wondering about that," I said, thinking of Master's family.

He frowned into the fire and cleared his throat. I was silenced. He continued, "Then, over a period of time, one particular group of people gained in strength and wealth until they became convinced that they were indeed better than all the other peoples, and set about by force to prove that and to rule over the whole world."

Jacks words became rushed, angry. "They possessed weapons, the like of which were unknown by most of the world, and their conquering march was almost unchallenged until they reached this same land upon which we live. Then a battle raged which almost destroyed the whole land, certainly, it changed the entire surface of it."

"The conquerors eventually declared themselves the victors," he continued. "After a battle lasting years that exacted an incredible toll in human life and suffering. A New Order was born. Those who had opposed the new leaders became workers and were kept in complete isolation from each other in small communities, much as Master's and...and others. They were not allowed to speak together, and the only communication was as you remember, quick, hurried and in secret."

"By the time the fighting had ended, a way of life had also ended. Once this entire land was covered with people and machines accomplished most of the work. The fighting destroyed most of the machines and annihilated the population."

"Small pockets of people, especially those in isolated areas were spared, mostly by accident, but some because of the lack of supplies and equipment towards the end of the fighting. Food became of vital necessity - many were dying from the lack of it - and because most of the industrial world had been destroyed, the small farms which sprang up had to be worked by hand - a slow and painful process to anyone not accustomed to working with their own skills."

"The state of the soil too, did not offer quick returns for their efforts. The fighting had rendered much of it sterile and to bring it back to a productive capacity would be the work of many years."

"Because of the situation in the most populated areas, no one could be spared to look for those who might have been missed, and there were no machines that would have aided the "Dominant Race" by travelling huge distances to find and destroy these small groups. Thus, they survived.

Water welled up in his eyes and began to trickle in a slow trail down his cheeks. "But most of the people in the land were overrun. Families were separated." Jack's voice became soft and wavering. "Children were torn from their parents and from each other and put into growing buildings across the land. Adults were assessed by their talents and put into labours which suited. Any sort of love or expressions of affection were completely rooted out of the worker's existence. There was no companionship, no communication. They did have education, were taught to read at a very young age, but the books they were given had been completely rewritten by the masters. The mention of anything that would encourage curiosity about themselves, their bodies, their social order, or any topic that was considered unnecessary or "dangerous" to the new order was completely removed."

"They were being programmed to become human machines - told what to learn, what to think, what to do and kept completely isolated from anyone who could have told them that

116

they were human beings and that there were certain inherent rights that went with that. Even the beautiful love that can be found between a husband and wife was taken away, along with the purest form of love of all, that of a mother and baby. That, too, was snatched from them and made into a simple mechanical act."

He went on. "Young females, upon reaching the age of twenty were admitted to "hospitals" where they were put to sleep and artificially inseminated."

I stared at him, uncomprehendingly.

"You have read how animals reproduce?"

I nodded.

"Well, you will find out sooner or later, but it is the same process for humans."

I felt my brows lower into a frown.

He sighed. "I know it is hard for you to understand, Liss," he said. "But bear with me. I promise it will be clear to you soon."

Again, I nodded.

"So the females would enter the hospital several times a year until they were 24 or until they became pregnant."

"You mean *carrying*."

He nodded. "Carrying a baby," he added. "If the former were the case, they would be retired and sold to a factory or workhouse. If the latter proved true, they would again be admitted to the hospital when the time drew near and the baby would be carefully removed through the stomach. The woman was stitched closed and the two separated - one to the growing buildings, the other to her place in the community, with only the scar and confused feelings to remind her of the experience."

I thought of the tiny young-one I had held so briefly, and the strong, confusing thoughts that had some to me and could only shake my head.

Jack paused and dabbed at his eyes with a soft, white cloth, which he pulled from a pocket in his robe. "Many babies— how many we'll never know—did not live through their first year

117

of life, though they were given plenty of nourishing food and kept clean and dry. I feel that they just wasted away through lack of love, for the workers assigned to the growing buildings were given strict rules concerning the amount of time to be spent with each child and what could be done in their service."

"The loss of these babies created constant demand for more and more to replenish the stock of workers as they were depleted—for the adults, too were dying through overwork and neglect or from sheer discouragement.

Thus a young female worker was to be prized and treated very well, until the time came when she was proven barren—then, unless she possessed remarkable talents which could prove useful to her master, she was sold without any hesitation."

Jack turned to look at me and I could see the shine of his moistened eyes in the firelight. "That was to be your fate, and I couldn't bear to see it happen," he said.

"I don't understand," I said. "Why was I different than the many other females at Master's?"

He reached out a gnarled hand and grasped my own. "To answer that I must tell another little story, and I don't think that I am up to that at this moment," he said. "It will be told—it must be told, but not now…not now."

He struggled to his feet, grunting a little as he did so. I stood with him and he clasped me in his arms for a moment and turned and walked toward his sleeping hut.

I remained by the fire, straining to see him through the darkness, even after the closing of a door told me that he had gone inside. Finally, I stooped and picked up my book, carrying it into the cooking house.

Everything was clean and neatly in its place so a cloth-draped plate sitting at the end of the table closest to the door was immediately noticeable. I lifted the cover and smiled as a plate of cold meats and vegetables was disclosed. "Mia," I said to myself, sitting down and pulling the plate towards me. I had almost finished eating when one of the doors opened and Mia stuck her head timidly into the opening.

"I see you found the food I saved you," she said softly, showing her beautiful, white teeth in an easy smile. I had watched her practice her smile in our mirror and it had by now become quite natural to her.

"I did, thank you very much," I smiled back at her. She pushed the door a little wider and moved into the room. As she approached the table, I saw her eyes drop to the book, which I had laid beside my plate.

"What are you reading now, Liss?" she asked.

"I found a book describing the Before Times," I answered. Her eyes widened. "Actually, it talks of the Before Times and also of what took place that changed everything from then to now."

"I just finished discussing it with Jack, too," I added. "I could not understand everything that he said, but I think that I have the right general idea and it is not easy to listen to."

Mia's huge dark eyes were fastened to my face. "The Before Times," she murmured, almost to herself. "That was when people knew what they were feeling, could put a name to it." She paused for a moment. Then she looked down at her hands twisted together in her lap. "That is what I would like to find out about more than anything else." She kept her eyes focussed on her hands. "I would like to know about feelings," she said softly. "I am ready now, I think, to understand them—and myself."

I thought of all that Jack had said—about the affection, the good and proper affection that had been so completely rooted out of the workers' lives, and I realised that what Jack had said some days ago was right. The masters had managed to eliminate any mention of it, but they had not managed to eliminate the feelings themselves.

Even though the workers could put no name or reason to their feelings, they were experienced.

CHAPTER FOURTEEN

At times, my aching head and tired eyes were more compelling than even my search for knowledge. It was at those times I would find Mia and spend the hours with her in the cooking house. Even with the language barriers that continued to hinder, many people guided us in the various techniques that went into producing the meals for the community. We were also introduced to Carol, a large and busy person who had charge of the weaving and sewing rooms, and who, we were happy to learn, spoke our language. She taught us how to make and dye the beautiful cloth and to construct the robes that were so common.

It was during those times, when our hands were occupied that we began to experiment with communication between ourselves. Our conversations were halting, at first, but soon we understood that no one was going to punish us for our thoughts and words and we spoke more and more freely.

One particular afternoon, a score or more of days after we had arrived, we were working at a well-scrubbed table which we had lugged outside under the trees. I was mixing a large batch of bread, still a slow process for me, and Mia was removing some very early peas from their shells.

She had been telling me about an unusually fine dish that she had prepared under Rebecca's tutelage and how fast it had disappeared when she had set it in front of a group of men on a trial basis. We had shared a laugh when she told of one young man who had risen with the empty plate in his hands and offered to do the cleaning up, only to learn with some dismay, that there were many dishes that had been soiled in the preparation of the treat.

I watched the way Mia's eyes sparkled as her laughter rippled and I realised that I was watching the face of a different person than the Mia who had arrived here with me only a short time ago. This was a person who found joy in being alive.

Happiness itself was such a new experience to us. We had felt a lift within us whenever we had accomplished something or were in the company of some peaceable companion. Sometimes, we had experienced good feelings at the end of a long and tiring day as we were served something that we found tasty, but we had never really understood what we were feeling or why. Our confusion was slowly becoming less and less painful to us with each passing day.

Here, we could experience emotions and were able to see what purpose they served. If we wished, we could even discuss them with people who had always acknowledged such things and could help us understand what we were feeling. As the days went by, I realised more and more what Jack must have gone through, knowing and understanding his feelings and having to suppress them merely to remain alive. For us it was a little easier. We had never known what we were feeling and could simply dismiss or ignore it until it disappeared.

Mia broke into my thoughts with a question that startled me.

"Liss, have you ever felt that you wanted to be with any one person?" she asked, timidly.

"I like to be with you, Mia," I said.

"Yes," she said, looking down at her hands and trying to scrape some of the green from under her nails. "I have put it badly. What I meant was…Have you ever felt your heart seem to jump right inside you when a certain person came into view? Have you ever wished … or…or she would come over and talk to you—just for a moment?"

My thoughts turned unwillingly to Young Master and I firmly brought them back, mentally chastising myself for my lack of control. "Yes, Mia," I said, looking across the settlement toward the trees lining the eastern wall. "It has happened to me, but only back at Master's—not with anyone here."

Her eyes seemed to light up at my words and I could tell that she was becoming very excited. "Oh, I'm so relieved!" she

121

exclaimed, throwing her hands into the air and almost upsetting her precious bowl of tiny green vegetables. Her next words were spoken rapidly, fairly falling from her lips in a jumble. "I have been watching the people here, and there are young couples who look at each other as though they are seeing something very special. Their hugs seem to be very different, somehow, and their smiles sort of…well…special."

"I even saw a young man and woman pressing their lips to the other's as I came around the corner of the cookhouse yesterday," she continued. "It was a strange sight, and it filled me with a strange, exciting feeling. For no reason at all, I found myself thinking of…someone." Her words trailed off and she pressed her hands suddenly to her cheeks and glanced quickly at me and then at the ground.

I was watching her with some interest and amusement, and found it difficult to suppress one of my newly discovered smiles. But I also felt relief—knowing that feelings that I had and could not explain were, perhaps, normal. I, too had seen several couples engaged in the salute that she had witnessed, and I had concluded that such an action was reserved only for the most special of acquaintances—an expression of the highest form of affection.

I bent over and studied her face closely. Mia's skin was so dark that it was difficult to tell for sure, but I was almost convinced that there was a red tinge to her cheeks, and I realised that she was feeling very uncomfortable.

"Who is it?" I whispered softly.

"Ross," she answered, even more softly.

I sat back, surprised at her answer. I should have seen it, or at the very least noticed some difference in the manner between the two of them. Then I realised that we were all so schooled in hiding any thought or feeling that for them to show anything, even to each other, would have been difficult indeed . . . and nearly impossible for anyone else to see. Now I smiled and touched her arm in the old two-fingered salute. "I am happy for you," I said, simply.

"But I don't know if he feels the same at all," she whispered. I had to lean over to hear the words. "How do I tell?"

She was asking the wrong person. I knew little about my own feelings and absolutely nothing about how to read anyone else's. Fortunately, I was saved from answering by Ross himself as he came around the corner of the cookhouse on the run and skidded to a halt beside us.

He gave me a formal greeting and then turned to look at Mia's bowed head. "Mia, please come, I have something to show you," he said, a little out of breath.

Ross had spent his days working with the cattle here, continuing with the same work for which he had been chosen at Master's. Now, however, he had discovered the pride found in doing ones best and the joy of sharing his accomplishments with others. He often came to tell us about something that was happening. He had been running and his body was wet with perspiration. His feet on the pathway had kicked up a fine film of dust that had layered itself over the moisture, making him look like a perfectly carved statue, and I could understand Mia's interest in him. But now the gleam in his dark eyes as they rested on Mia's bowed form was unmistakable and I caught my breath.

I could tell! Ross did care for Mia—as much as she cared for him, and I could tell! It was written for all to see in the eyes!

Mia raised her head and the colour was now very apparent in her face. "Of course," she said, "We'd enjoy that very much." They both turned to look at me.

"Oh," I stuttered. "Um, well…I…uh…I really do have to finish mixing this bread," I said, pounding down into the mass of brown dough with both fists and trying to look very busy. "You two go along."

Mia needed no urging and rose quickly and gracefully to her feet. Then she followed Ross on the run along the pathway toward the barns where the cowherd was housed.

As they disappeared from sight, I looked down at my hands, watching them knead the dough as if they belonged to someone else. I lifted them and rubbed them together to remove the tiny rolls of bread that clung to them. Then I spread a clean cloth over the bowl and carried it into the cookhouse, placing it near the huge brick ovens where it could be warmed and would rise.

Rebecca was checking a joint of meat cooking for the evening meal and she greeted me as I came in. I smiled at her as I left the bowl, then turning, I made my way back to the table outside. I seated myself and prepared to finish Mia's peas.

A few minutes later, Rebecca joined me. I looked up at her as she brushed off a corner of the table and sat down. "Where Mia?" she asked, looking around.

"With Ross," I answered, smiling.

"Ah," she said, smiling back and turning to look in the direction of the barns. She shaded her eyes for a moment, then turned back to me. Of all the people here, Rebecca had made the most concerted attempts to visit with us and to learn some of our language. I had thought her progress nothing short of amazing until I was told that she had a little of our language before we came. She could talk to us quite freely now, and it was from her that we had learned most of the ways of the people. "How you feel?" she asked now.

"Fine, strong," I answered, flexing a rather sorry-looking and very slender arm.

"No, no. How you feel about Ross and Mia?"

Was I the last to realise that there were feelings between the two, I wondered? I looked into Rebecca's brown eyes. "I feel good," I said, smiling.

"Good," she answered. "Long time happening."

"Yes," I said. At least a score of days, I thought to myself.

"Feelings start before you come here." She surprised me. "Mia hear Ross go with Jack. Mia go with Ross."

So that was how it happened. She had felt these things back at Master's. I wondered how long they had been puzzling her. Almost as long as my feelings for Young Master had been puzzling me, probably. And in that instant, everything was suddenly clear. I kept thinking about Young Master because I cared for him. I cared for him like Mia cared for Ross. A worker for a master.

I must have lost my mind.

CHAPTER FIFTEEN

The days sped by. Always I was busy with some task, or, increasingly, with my precious books. Even as I drove myself to learn more and more, I knew deep inside that it was no longer the search for knowledge, but escape from reality that I sought. I feared that my newfound feelings could never serve any purpose and now that I could finally understand what I felt, I was unable to do anything about it.

Ross and Mia spent most of the days together, either at the barns or working in the kitchens. They seemed to never lack things to say to each other, and this surprised me, for they had both been raised as I had and talking did not come easy to any of us.

I began to avoid them and their happiness, angry with myself even as I did so. I hid more and more in the library, grateful to have something that would occupy my mind and shut out the pain that increased with each day. But as I soaked in the knowledge, village life went on about me and some interesting developments began to take place.

One morning, I had just settled into my favourite spot in the little hut and pulled out the book that I was interested in at the moment when a light rapping sounded at the door. In surprise, I looked up just as the door swung slowly inwards. Mia and Ross stood just outside.

"Can we come in, Liss?" asked Mia.

"Of course," I answered, wondering as I did so what could bring them to the library now? They had shown little interest in it before.

"We wanted to tell you first," Mia said softly, looking at Ross and reaching for his hand. "Ross and I are going to marry."

"Marry?" I asked stupidly.

"Do you understand what we are saying, Liss?" Ross asked, looking from Mia to me, "Do you know what marriage means?"

I had read of marriage in several different books and I had heard Jack speak of it. I knew that it meant the joining together, mentally, emotionally and physically of two persons. Two persons who then became one in spirit and purpose. Yes, I knew what marriage was. The thought of it made me ache inside.

I forced a smile for the two of them, then laid my book down and rose to give each of them a hug. "I am pleased for you," I said. "Apparently I have missed out on much in the past few days."

"We have spent a lot of time with the other young couples, talking to them and watching them," Ross said, looking down at Mia. "We have been taught a lot of what we will need to know about our own feelings, and about marriage. We feel that we are prepared to take this step." Mia looked up at him, and the glance they shared was beautiful to see. This idea of marriage seemed to make a person complete, somehow.

Once again I thought of Young Master, but only for a moment.

"When is this to take place?" I asked.

"We see no need to wait for a long period," Mia said. "The village Elder will perform the ceremony in seven days."

"Seven days," I echoed. "Isn't there a lot to accomplish in that time?" I thought of weddings I had read about in my books – beautiful clothing, complex ceremonies, extensive arrangements. But then I realised that this was to be a simple ceremony and neither the planning nor the arrangements would be difficult and could easily be accomplished half that time. "What do you need me to do?"

The days had passed quickly before, but now they flew by. There was not a lot that needed to be done, but what there was took some time. Rebecca took care of the arrangements for the wedding feast, and the robe that Mia would wear was in the capable hands of Carol. Both of these women had gained their positions because of their skill, so we knew that whatever they put their hands to, would be perfect.

All that remained before the young couple could marry was to find them a place to live. This concerned me. I even wondered if I should offer them our cabin. Whenever I approached the subject with Mia however, she would just smile and shrug her shoulders. I even tried to discuss it with Jack, but he told me it would be taken care of according to custom.

I was silenced.

During those days before the wedding, I made a discovery. When a very capable person takes control of a project, there is not much room for the help of an amateur. After I had been told for about the fourth time that there really was not anything I could help with, I gave up and retreated to my books, and there I made another discovery.

When Life is progressing at its usual unhurried pace, books can supply much needed excitement. But when life breaks into a forward run and the events are happening almost too fast, trying to concentrate on a printed page can become torture.

I spent my days at the library, but I did not learn much.

Just before sunrise on the day of the wedding, all the men of the village gathered together beside the northernmost cottages. They had assembled huge stacks of sweet-smelling lumber and were busily sorting and talking together. The grass and topsoil in one space had been peeled back and a rectangle of huge timbers had been sunk deeply into the earth. The women were clustered in groups around the edge of the area and had their heads together laughing and talking animatedly. Children ran screaming to and fro, getting in the men's way and startling the women. But their high spirits only seemed to add to the excitement and the adults watched them mostly with indulgent amusement.

Suddenly the crowd hushed and Ramannah in all her finery floated gracefully between the groups of women until she had reached the area where the lumber was piled. Then she turned.

"This great day," she said sombrely. "Mia and Ross choose this day for wedding day."

It registered, dimly, that she was speaking in our language and that everyone seemed to understand, but at the moment, I was more interested in watching Ross come out from among the group of men.

Mia left the smiling group of women and joined him beside Ramannah. She grasped their hands and joined them together, then, still holding them, she turned back to the crowd.

Jack quietly came up beside me.

"Wedding ceremony starts now with building of family shell. Ross and Mia will then fill shell and make it home." She looked towards the eastern rim of the valley. The sun was just touching the edge of the cliff. "We will pray."

One of the men of the village moved beside her and dipped his head and squeezed his eyes shut. As one, the villagers copied his actions.

I was slowly becoming accustomed to the villagers' 'prayers', which they seemed to do at all times and for every occasion, but, still, I turned to Jack, questions on my lips.

"Shhh," he said, silencing me.

"God, our Father," the man said, "Please bless us, this day. Please bless this couple as they begin their life together." He paused and I looked around, thinking he was finished. But heads around me remained tipped. He went on, his voice shaky. "Bless them, Father, with health. With work. With children in due course. With joy and happiness in each other. With continued peace and freedom. Amen."

The rest of the crowd repeated that last word. And I suddenly remembered that first prayer, said in the people's own language, on the day we had first joined them. I finally knew what was being said. Though not the reason why.

"They are speaking with their God," Jack whispered. "Asking Him for peace and protection."

129

"Oh," I whispered back. I still did not understand. Who was this *God*, that they would petition him so?

Ramannah had lifted her head. "Let the day begin!" she commanded.

Everyone cheered and turned at once to an assigned task, some labouring at the site itself, and some busy at separate projects alongside. I was carefully instructed as to what I should do by a young man of about 12 years.

From then on, I was kept busy supplying small pegs of wood – used to fasten everything together – to different groups.

Men and women worked side by side throughout the morning. The floor appeared almost magically, and was immediately supporting four skeletal walls.

I realised that owing to the haste necessary in the building, groups were actually putting the walls together beside the house site and then they were merely lifted into place when the time came. It was all amazingly swift and efficient.

Almost before the walls were fastened down, the roof was being lifted into place. The doorways and windows could be seen, and I could imagine what the finished product would look like. Then, as the sun stood at its highest in the sky, the women disappeared for a short time while the men continued their labours.

I left my piles of lumber and followed the women to the cookhouse. Someone handed me a huge platter of freshly baked breads. I walked quickly back to the building site with it and laid it down with the other dishes that had appeared there. Then, talking and laughing, the people gathered around and sat on the soft grass.

Ross and Mia sat together on Ramannah's right and Jack and I took our places on her left. One of the men stood and said a few words with his head bowed humbly. He was, once more, speaking in their tongue. I was startled to realize that I was beginning to understand a little of their language. I recognized requests for continued freedom and appreciation for having plenty to eat. He finished and sat down and the meal began.

I turned to Jack. "Explain it all to me," I demanded.

Jack smiled broadly and turned to me. "Explain what?" he asked innocently.

"You know," I said. "Explain what has been happening here…please."

He laughed aloud and threw an arm around my shoulders, giving them a quick squeeze. "They have many customs here," he began. "This is one of the most special—the ceremony of the Wedding. Whenever a couple decides to marry, the whole village becomes involved. The needs to be met are simple—food, clothing and shelter. Everyone helps with everything that must be done."

"The best part of all is the actual wedding day. As you have observed, the village must construct a house for the young couple. It must be completed between sunrise and sunset. As soon as it is finished, the actual wedding ceremony may take place. Then the new marrieds return to their new home. It is their first night together and in their new home and in their new life."

He looked at me, "As all the customs you will find here, it is very simple and very beautiful."

"It is beautiful," I said softly. "I realise now that I had understood most of what was happening, but it is nice to have it explained." I suddenly noticed that everyone had finished eating. Many had risen and were returning to their work.

I helped Rebecca and a few of the women collect the now-empty platters and carry them to the cookhouse. We cleaned them, and then I wandered back to the activity.

The skeleton of the building was being covered with large pieces of logs, sliced lengthways and fitted closely together. I watched as one of the men trimmed the sides of each piece so it would fit very snugly to the one below it. Even as the walls were

131

going up, another of the men was fitting a door into the space provided for it, swinging it back and forth on oiled leather hinges.

Several of the women were busy at a large trough on the far side of the site and I wandered over for a closer look. Two men and some of the larger children were hauling black soil from a spot near the river in buckets and dumping the contents into the large wooden apparatus. Then buckets of water and armloads of clean straw were added, the whole tromped into a thick, dark mass by several exuberant children, the girls holding robes above their knees, and the boys spraying mud everywhere, much to the amusement of those watching.

As soon as the mixture reached a certain consistency, the women would scrape it into several buckets where it was hauled over to the house.

One of the walls had already been completed and several villagers started scooping handfuls of the mixture over the new wall, spreading it with flat, wooden tools into a thick coating.

They worked smoothly and carefully, making certain that every inch of surface was given an equal cover. I realised that this would be very effective at sealing the newly constructed walls against both moisture and wind, once the coating was well dried.

Another wall was closed in and the mud crew spread out to finish that wall, too.

The roof was almost completely covered by this time, and I was watching to see if the people would be hauling buckets of the dark, smelly mud to the top of the house when I heard the sound of someone hollering at a team and the jangle of harness. I turned just as Ross and a small crew appeared through the trees with a team pulling a sledge. The team was labouring hard and I realised that they were hauling a load of thick strips of soil, with the grass still clinging to them.

Ross halted the team near the almost completed house and I saw moisture—tears—sparkle in his eyes for a moment at he viewed the construction. Then he was busy, unloading the sledge and hauling the grass strips up on to the roof.

Curious, I followed him, climbing nimbly until I could get a good view of this newest enterprise. The first strips of grass were being laid firmly along the very outer edges of the roof and I knelt down for a closer view. A small ridge kept each of these pieces from sliding off. The workers carefully fitted in more and more, until the whole roof looked just like the fields, which stretched out on all sides. I almost expected one of the village's cows to come strolling over the top, looking for just the right tidbit to chew. I climbed down.

The mud crew was completing their third wall by this time and several women were hanging the shutters that would close out the world during cool or stormy weather. When these tasks had been completed, everyone stood back and viewed the day's labours.

"It still lacks the fireplace," Jack said, coming up to me. "It and the rest of the fourth wall will not be mudded until that can be completed, but the cabin can now be lived in until cooler weather."

I turned and smiled my thanks at him just as a cheer broke out. Everyone was hugging and slapping backs and jumping in sheer joy.

Ross and Mia were standing together, looking up at the day's accomplishments. Mia was crying softly. I could see the tears make tiny dots on the front of her robe and I saw Ross' eyes glisten suspiciously.

There was a small moment of silence, then Ross and Mia were separated, escorted to their separate cabins and the doors shut. As soon as they were out of sight, everyone scattered. I started to make my way over to my cabin to see if Mia wanted my help with anything.

I realised that I knew very little about what was going on. Every night, Mia had spent the hours between supper and bedtime with Ross, only coming back to sleep. I was usually already in bed and drowsy when she came in, so though she was quite ready to talk, I took in very little of what she said. Now I was feeling a little left out and more than a little sorry for myself.

Thoughts of Young Master had flitted in and out of my mind all day, too. I just hadn't been able to keep them away. My feelings for him were so strong but at the same time, so useless. Mia's happiness made my own life seem, somehow, futile.

I knew what I was feeling was pure selfishness, but I could not seem rid myself of it.

I shook myself, mentally. If I couldn't forget him and my own silly life, at least I could put my problems aside and help Mia enjoy her day. I started to move more purposefully toward the cabin.

Suddenly, people began to appear from different buildings all over the village. They carried strange bundles and packages and were heading toward Ross and Mia's newly completed cabin. I turned and followed them in curiosity.

Peering through one of the windows, I could see some of the women hanging curtains and other people setting up a new bed - much larger than either of those found in our cabin. Two men laid a new mattress down and several women shook out new linens, crisply, startlingly white, and smoothed them over the bed, tucking them in neatly at the corners.

Carol came bustling in with an enormous bundle clutched tightly in her arms.

She said something to the others there, and I caught a little about having to hurry before she shoved the bundle into the arms of the nearest man and scurried back out the door. He turned and tossed the bundle on the bed. It burst open to disclose the most beautiful quilt I have ever seen.

It was in small patches in every colour imaginable, worked into an intricate pattern. One of the women shook it out and spread it across the bed and several of us gasped as she did so. Truly it was a work of art.

Carol had cut pieces of material and sewed them neatly into pictures. At the center was a man, a woman, and several children. I realized—with a pang, and the briefest of thoughts about Young Master—that I was looking at a family.

Behind them was their home, almost identical to the one just completed. And surrounding them on every side were friends and relatives, the village, even the cowherd. It was like a glimpse into the future of Ross and Mia's life together. It was also a sign that they were truly a part of the village.

I took a short, sharp breath.

Rebecca slipped through the door. Seeing me, she came over. "You feel a little sad, a little happy?" she asked.

"Exactly!" I said in surprise. How had she known? Was I that obvious?

"It is normal," she answered, putting her arms around me and giving me a hug. "Come, now, we are almost ready."

Normal? Suddenly I didn't feel bad at all. I wasn't being selfish. Wel…maybe I was, but it was normal. It would pass.

I ran to the cabin.

CHAPTER SIXTEEN

The next hours are a blur in my mind. I remember entering my cabin expecting to see the bride, but finding it empty. For a moment, I stood in the centre of the room, confused. Then I decided that Mia must be dressing at Carol's cabin or the sewing house further down the street.

I poured water into a basin and washed quickly, using tepid water from my bucket on the floor. Then I smoothed my hair carefully in front of the mirror, discarded my soiled robes and donned clean. Taking one last look in the mirror, I left the cabin.

People were already gathering in the centre of the village. I ran over to them. A box-like structure, completely covered in a soft, white material, had been erected on the soft grass, and a slender, white rope entwined with tiny, white flowers, had been strung completely around it.

Entrance to the enclosure was only through a narrow corridor, also formed by the beautifully decorated ropes, which led from the eastern side of the village.

The people were seating themselves as close to the barriers as they could get and were talking and laughing quietly. The mood was different now. Everyone seemed happy, but hushed, as though this was a wonderful, but respectful, occasion.

The sun had set and the shadows were lengthening, though the area in which we were assembled remained quite light. It was not long before the entire population of the village was assembled, with parents holding their little ones and speaking quietly to them—perhaps explaining what was happening.

I suddenly wished that I had someone to explain it to me. I looked around for Jack, but couldn't see him.

During the past few days, I had begun to be more and more uncomfortable in the presence of the children. At meal-times or any other time when it was necessary for us to be in contact with each-other, I always found myself wanting to take them on my lap and cuddle them, especially the very tiny ones. They seemed to constantly bring me to the brink of tears, simply by looking at me, or even by standing too close.

To alleviate these strange feelings, I had begun avoiding all children. Until I could safely deal with my emotions, I felt that distance was my safest choice.

A little girl was seated with her mother next to me, and I desperately tried to ignore them both. Deliberately, I concentrated on a conversation taking place on the other side of me.

Suddenly, a small cloth ball landed in my lap. I picked it up and was examining it when the tiny girl followed it. She sat down comfortably and reached for her ball.

I handed it to her and waited for her to leave, but she settled more comfortably and turned to watch the people, content to stay in my lap. I turned to look at her mother, who smiled at me and nodded. Unwillingly and almost of their own accord, my arms went around the tiny body, and I hugged her tight to me.

For a moment, tears threatened. I took a deep breath, swallowed hard and blinked rapidly for a few moments. Finally, I gained a modicum of control.

Then I, too settled to watch.

A hush fell over the crowd and Ramannah, again in her finery, floated up the narrow corridor and seated herself on the far side of the box from where we waited.

Then the crowd rose to its feet. Lifting the little girl in my arms, I too, struggled to stand.

Mia and Ross, their arms linked together, stood just outside the corridor of ropes. Behind them, one of the village elders hovered. I recognised him. He was Ramannah's husband, Kai.

My eyes were drawn to Mia's robes and I gasped. They were a marvellous, glistening white, almost too bright and shining to look upon without narrowing my eyes. Ross was dressed in a like manner, in white. Their clothing made their dark skin look almost ebony in colour and the two of them were incredibly beautiful to see.

Tiny white flowers had been entwined in Mia's hair and she carried a huge bunch of the same blossoms in her free left hand. She caught my eye and nodded to me, flashing her wonderful smile.

Suddenly, my happiness for her overshadowed all else.

The two of them began to walk down the corridor toward the altar, taking slow, measured steps. They were followed, not too closely, by Kai. Reaching the small compound, Ross walked Mia around to the far side of the box, where she sank to her knees. Then he knelt opposite her.

Kai took his place at the head of the box, in front of Ramannah, and cleared his throat. He nodded to the crowd and we sank back to the soft grass, straining to hear every word spoken.

I remember little now of what he said, though great pains were taken to speak in our language. Kai spoke of caring for each other always, even if circumstances should change, and of welcoming little children to their home.

What I do remember clearly is the expression that shone on Mia's face. She kept her eyes on Ross, even as she responded to questions asked by the elder. I realised that I was looking at the face of someone who cared more for another person than for anything else in existence, including herself.

It made my heart thump queerly in my chest and I found myself studying Ross, wondering if he was experiencing something similar.

Finally, Kai took their hands and joined them together over the box. They were instructed to kiss as man and wife. Ross leaned forward and pressed his lips briefly to Mia's and then they rose to their feet, still clutching each other's hands. They edged away from the box and turned together towards us.

Everyone rose to their feet once more, and I hefted the little girl into one arm and pressed my other hand to the ground to steady myself so I, too could stand. Ross and Mia walked slowly back down the corridor and stood at the end of it. There, they received the congratulations of the whole village.

As soon as they had hugged and kissed the bride and groom, several of the older children raced off towards the barns and outbuildings. A few of the men followed them.

Soon, rising over the trees I could see huge balloons, in many colours. I suddenly remembered our arrival and I realised that the people were again celebrating— sending their joy and happiness aloft with their balloons.

The children still standing with their parents screamed with excitement and pointed to the sky, shouting to their neighbours and their parents as more and more of the balloons drifted skyward.

The people standing about me were abuzz with the wonder of everything, and everyone divided their time between hugging and crying over the newly-married couple and marvelling over the bright balls disappearing into the early evening sky.

The children had a very difficult time deciding whether they would rather watch the balloons or congratulate the bride and groom. Many of them tried both, hugging a leg or waist or whatever happened to be at their level and twisting about to keep at least one eye on the sky.

The little girl in my arms made a dive for her mother and I relinquished her and walked over for my turn to congratulate Ross and Mia.

Looking into their eyes, I was astonished at the peace I saw. They were entirely content with their life and with each other. I gave each of them a hug and my congratulations and turned away, surprised to find tears on my cheeks.

When everyone had congratulated them at least once—and some two or three times—the crowd pushed the couple towards the trees lining the river. It was growing quite dark by this time, and the balloons had long since disappeared. Those who had launched them had re-joined the crowd and the long shadows seemed to swallow us all as we entered the woods.

Passing through the line of trees, we found that a huge feast had been prepared and laid out on a long white cloth along the banks of the river. Ross and Mia were seated at one end of the cloth, and Ramannah and Kai took places opposite. Lanterns had been hung from the trees, and cast a soft orange glow over the area.

Ramannah nodded and another of the village elders moved forward and bowed his head, offering thanks for the beautiful blessing of marriage and for the abundant blessings of celebrating with such plenty, and again, speaking slowly in my tongue. Then he took his place and the whole village did the same.

I found myself once more beside Jack, who was seated next to Ramannah, and, to my surprise, a young man of the village took the place on my other side, smiling at me shyly. I smiled briefly at him and then turned my attention to the food set out before me.

An entire side of beef had been roasted and was now laying on a bed of green leaves in the centre of the long cloth. Rich juices were oozing from it and running along to drip slowly into the green bed and the white cloth below. The meat was entirely surrounded by platters of vegetables in every colour from palest yellow to deepest orange and in every hue of green.

Breads of every description - braided, twisted, rolled, or simply baked in a long loaf and sliced - lay in delicately browned heaps. Small pots of butter and honey flanked them.

Fruit dishes had been set all along the outer edges of the cloth and steamed quietly, breathing the scent of apples, plums, peaches and spices into the air. I wanted to taste everything at once.

Indeed, I had great difficulty in choosing what I would try first. I was still totally absorbed in my dinner sometime later, when Jack leaned closer to me.

"You need to try to mix with the people a little more," he said.

I looked at him in surprise. "What do you mean?"

"You spend far too much time in the library or by yourself," he said, looking down at his plate and breaking a twist of bread apart with his long fingers. "You need to spend more of your time with the people. You must learn some of their ways."

"I thought I was learning," I said, slowly. "That is why I read so much. I have a thirst to know everything."

"I understand why you read, but you can only learn so much from a printed page," he said. "You must learn the rest from the people. You must become a friend."

I looked up in astonishment. "But I am a friend, I am!"

"Perhaps I worded it wrong." He patted my arm. "What I meant was that you must take a little more time to learn the customs and ways of a free person. You must ask more questions, talk to me, to others. You must have realised by now that most of them understand and even speak a little of our language. They would very much like to help you—to get to know you. You are clinging to your worker's ways—living within yourself, sorting out answers to your own questions. It isn't necessary and can mislead you."

"I am afraid I really do not understand what you mean." I was feeling more and more confused, and forgetting for the moment that I had been only too grateful for explanations as recently as this noon. "I have always had to answer my own questions. I am used to doing it that way."

"But it isn't necessary," he said. "Now you have the opportunity to discuss anything that confuses you with the people around you, to enjoy the company of other humans, to be really happy."

I looked at Mia and Ross. They spent hours in the company of the villagers learning the ways of free people. And they were happy. "I want to be happy," I murmured.

Jack had to bend low to hear the quiet words. He smiled. "Then start learning," he said, indicating the young man who sat beside me.

But I still wasn't ready. I knew that one reason I clung to my old ways was because of my thoughts about Young Master, though Jack could not know this. Numbly, I turned and smiled at the young man. "Hello."

"Good evening, Liss," he said.

"Oh…" He had taken me by surprise. "You know my name."

"Everyone does," he said, smiling.

"Oh," was all I could get out.

"I am Isaac," he said.

"It is very pleasant to meet you," I said, politely.

"Thank you," he responded. "And it is very nice to finally get to meet you!"

As Isaac said these words, I happened to catch Jack's eye. He was smiling at me, nodding in an 'I told you so' manner.

And so our conversation went. Both of us struggling for something to say, and one of us, at least, very uncomfortable.

Suddenly, we were saved by movement from the head of the gathering. Ross and Mia had risen to their feet and Ramannah and Kai had moved around to stand behind them.

A young woman brought a tiny infant and laid it in Mia's arms. Even from where I sat, I could see the tears sparkle in Mia's eyes as she cuddled it close to her. A hush fell over the crowd.

"And so it will be," Ramannah said, indicating the baby held so tenderly. "Now go and start your new life together."

Mia handed the tiny one back to its mother, then she reached for Ross' hand and the two of them made their way alone along the pathway through the trees. They soon were gone from our sight but I could picture them walking slowly through the deserted village to their cottage.

The tears, once more, spilled down my cheeks.

Several of the villagers had arisen and were preparing to play drums and hand-carved instruments for dancing. I had grown accustomed to their love of showing happiness and enthusiasm in this manner, but I wasn't feeling like joining in tonight. I excused myself. I could feel Jack's eyes on me and I knew that he must be disappointed in me, but I could not help it. I had to be alone with my thoughts. Slowly I made my way to my cabin and closed the door, leaning against it briefly before lighting the lamp.

Mia's possessions had all been removed and the room seemed somehow empty without them there. I was surprised at my thoughts. All my life, I had lived alone. I had found it strange to have someone else share the same room. Now with that person gone, I was missing her presence. Once again, I did not understand myself.

I walked over to the mirror and peered at my face, reaching for my hairbrush and running it through my hair—preparing to retire without being conscious of my movements.

Suddenly, my hand dropped to my side and I was seeing Ross and Mia standing at the head of the gathering with the tiny baby in Mia's arms. This was it. This was how life was supposed to be lived, within the circle of a family's love. This was what counted.

I thought of Young Master and my feelings for him. I knew in that moment that my future was somehow a part of his future. That in some way, I had to convince him to come here with me, to marry me and be the father of our children. To forget the old ways and create new ones that were older still.

My thoughts turned suddenly to Meg for the first time in days and I realised by counting the weeks that she probably had been delivered of her baby by now. That she had been "marked" as I had once called it, and that her baby had been taken away from her and was, even now, in a growing building and perhaps dying from lack of love.

The urgency in my own behalf was very strong, but it was eclipsed by these new thoughts. I knew that the time had come. I had to go back. Perhaps the first thing I would lose would be my freedom and then all would be lost in turn, but I knew that I had to try. For Meg and her baby…for Young Master…and for myself.

PART THREE

CHAPTER SEVENTEEN

I awoke early the next morning, in spite of the fact that I hadn't been able to close my eyes for hours after retiring. The thoughts had whirled around chaotically until I was dizzy. Finally, after tossing about for several hours, I had reached a decision and my mind had stilled. Though the music and laughter had continued to drift through my open window for the rest of the night, my thoughts were at peace and I was able to release my hold on consciousness.

I arose and groomed myself for the day, and then left my room in search of breakfast. I thought of the huge meal that I had eaten only a few hours before and was amazed that I could be hungry again so soon, but hungry, I was, and I needed something now.

The village was abnormally quiet this morning. Usually by this time, though it was early, the men were leaving for the fields and the women were tending to their village duties or their little ones or their cabins, or even gathering in small groups for a few minutes talk. Today, most of the doors were still tightly shut and only one or two people greeted me on my walk to the cooking building.

I pushed open the door of the place that should have been alive with activity, only to be met with utter silence. I glanced around, unsurprised to find that, in spite of the late meal and the celebrations that went into the night, Rebecca and her crew had cleaned everything to its usual shine.

I walked over to the north wall of the room and reached down to grasp a huge metal ring set into the floor. Pulling hard, I lifted a trap door and set it back upon the floor. I had seen Rebecca do this several days earlier, as I was finishing a solitary meal. She had then carried a large platter of uneaten foods down into the disclosed recess.

I had followed and was given a tour of the storage cellars of the village.

I glanced around. Seeing a lantern swinging from a hook and glowing slightly, I grabbed it and held it up, illuminating the steep steps. I made my way cautiously down into the blackness below. Reaching the bottom, I lifted the lantern high and continued along a narrow corridor which ended at a heavy door.

Rebecca had explained the construction and importance of these unique tunnels. They had been completely lined with stones hauled from the banks of the river several miles upstream, and were very cool. Perfect for the storage, and temporary preservation of all types of food.

The only problem with them was their tendency towards dampness. Rebecca and her crew were constantly wiping down the walls and scrubbing the floors, and though the wet still seeped in, it was minimal, and the continual cleaning ensured that there were no bugs and very few mice.

I swung the heavy door open and set my lamp on a table nearby. On some shelves in front of me were great bowls covered with clean, bright cloths. Peeping into several, I discovered breads and vegetables left over from the previous day's celebrations, all carefully preserved. I walked over to another shelf and took down a clean plate and a large spoon and dished food from several of the bowls. I found that some of the meat had also been left over and was wrapped in moist cloths on yet another shelf. I pulled off a couple of pieces and placed them between two slices of soft bread. Then I picked up my plate and the lantern and retraced my steps, pushing the door shut with my foot as I passed through.

Rebecca was standing at the top of the stairs when I emerged. She had both hands on her hips and looked quite belligerent until she recognised me.

"Oh Liss," she said in her tentative English, reaching for the lantern that I held. "I do not know who down in cellar. I angry."

"I am sorry, Rebecca," I said quietly. "I was just so hungry, I couldn't wait for breakfast. And everyone seemed to be sleeping late this morning."

"It always so after celebrations," Rebecca said, nodding. "Everyone dance late, then sleep late." She glanced down at the laden plate that I carried and smiled. "Take food out. Eat in sunshine."

I obeyed and sat down on the soft grass near the square. The white, box-like structure was still sitting in the center of the area, and the ropes still stretched around it, though the flowers were a little wilted by now. It still looked beautiful to me, however, and the thoughts that had been uppermost during the ceremony and afterwards, returned.

I finished my plateful of food, though I was so deep in thought that I hardly tasted any of it. Then I cleaned my plate and spoon at the pump beside the cookhouse and carried them back into the building. Rebecca must have gone down into the cellar herself, because she was not in sight when I entered but the trap door was still open.

Some of the men and women assigned to help her were beginning to assemble and were dragging out dishes and pots, ready to start breakfast preparations. I smiled at them and left.

The sun was far up in the sky by this time, and was already quite warm. I walked over to one of the huge trees that stood in the square and sat down with my back next to the rough trunk. From there, I watched the village come to life.

Doors all down the street were opening and men and women were carrying large buckets to the river. From there, they returned to their cottages and soon freshly scrubbed children were leaving the small huts and racing around in the sunshine. I watched a group of them playing a complicated game with balls and a circle drawn in the dirt and smiled at the shouts and laughter that seemed to be a part of the game.

Suddenly someone came to the door of the cook house and hollered. Balls and game were abandoned as hungry children raced madly toward their breakfasts.

The villagers made their way singly and in groups toward the building, talking contentedly with each other. Jack was right. I had read many of the books available in the library and had learned many things, but I had never spent enough time with the people in the village. I knew almost nothing about them or their daily existence. In recent days, I had even taken my meals in the library, thus denying myself such simple opportunities for learning as studying the people when they gathered to eat.

Even now, I stayed where I was, only shifting my position when I got uncomfortable. Soon, the people began to file out of the building, and I knew that the meal was over and that everyone would soon be beginning their day's labours.

But again, I was wrong. During the weeks that we had been here, I had observed that on every seventh day, only the essential jobs were completed—cooking, eating, caring for the animals. I had lost track of the days of the week, but now I realised that this must be a seventh day. The people were in no hurry, but rather, gathered together in small groups and engaged in what appeared to be their favourite pastime, visiting.

The area slowly filled with the talking, laughing crowd, until it seemed that the whole village had gathered to enjoy the morning sunshine.

Suddenly a hush fell over the crowd and I realised that Ross and Mia had left their cabin and were strolling slowly toward a belated breakfast. His arm was about her shoulders and he whispered something in her ear. She looked up at him and laughed. They seemed to be completely relaxed and happy merely to be in each other's company.

Many of the villagers greeted them as they passed and a few ran forward to give each of them a hug. Then the couple disappeared into the building and those gathered in the square returned to their conversations.

Jack came out of the cook house and spotted me sitting there. He came over. "Well, Liss," he said, smiling broadly at me. "And how are you this beautiful morning?"

I looked up at him. It was a shame to give him such a shock so early on such a beautiful day, but...

I sighed. "I am going back," I said to him.

It took him a moment to realise what I had said, and I watched, almost in amusement, the play of expressions across his seamed face. The pleasant look he wore faded, and surprise, puzzlement, fear, and finally, sadness chased each other across his brow. He looked up toward the cliffs, which hemmed us in on the east. "I was afraid that you would come to that decision," he said softly, sinking to the grass beside me. "I thought if you could become interested in one of the young men here, that you would settle down and stay. Is it Meg you are missing, or is it...another reason?"

"I am in love with Young Master," I said, looking down at my feet. There. It had been said. It was out in the open. But I wasn't prepared for his reaction.

Jack reached out and grabbed my upper arms in a painful grip. "A master! Oh no, Liss. No! Please say you are making some sort of terrible joke! Please tell me anything but that!"

"It is true," I said quietly, moving my arms to free them. "And I have to go back."

He looked at me and I was astonished at his ravaged features. He looked like he had received a terrible blow. Then his face got quite white and his lips turned the colour of clay.

I jumped to his side. "Jack!" I said urgently. "Are you all right?" I pushed his head forward onto his knees.

Soon his colour began to return and he was able to sit up. He looked at me, rather dazedly. Then his face cleared and he again grabbed my arm. "Liss, do you know what you are saying?" he demanded.

"Yes, Jack, I do. I have lain awake most of the night and thought it through. You and the wonderful people here have taught me to feel, or at least to understand what I am feeling. You have shown me love, and how to express love. But at the same time, I have come to the realisation that my heart was awakened back at Master's and has remained there, with Young Master. I cannot be happy without him."

I took a deep breath and let it out slowly. "If it means that I give up my freedom to be near him, that I will probably watch him grow and take a wife and raise a family, all without ever knowing what I feel for him, so be it. I have to spend my life near him. It is the only way that I can be happy."

"Only the strong souls survive the growing buildings," Jack murmured, almost to himself. He looked at me. "And you are one of the strongest. But it will not be the same. You understand your feelings now, you can be hurt and you can feel anger and frustration. Do you really think you can cope?"

"I *will* cope," I said simply.

"Oh, Liss, I could wish you all the happiness in the world, if you were leaving for any other reason than this. But if you must follow your heart—even into utter destruction, I will not stand in your way!" He glanced down at his hands for a moment. Then he looked back at me. "But before we make our arrangements to leave, I have to tell you a story. Perhaps, even yet, you will change your mind."

"Jack!" I only caught part of what he said. "You said 'our arrangements'! Do you mean that you will…"

"Hush now, child, and listen." Jack moved over until he could rest his back against the trunk of the tree, and side-by-side, we sat there. "This story goes back almost ninety years, but I must start at the beginning," he said.

"I was born and raised to young manhood in a village not unlike this, though we had a few modern conveniences. Everyone worked together, loved, married, raised children and died without ever setting foot outside the borders of their own village. Oh, an occasional boy or girl met someone from another place and escaped there, but most of the villagers stayed, generation after generation."

"My father wanted more than that for me. Many times he had seen me watch the great planes fly overhead, and often we had spoken of my love for the wonders of the air. One day, he arranged a trip for himself and I to a large city a day's drive from the village and while there, he took me to an airport—a place where those great machines took off and landed."

Jack looked up into the sky, his face serene. "I'll never forget my first glimpse of the place. It was like a dream come true. I loved the sights, the sounds, even the smells. From that moment, I knew that I wanted to spend my life with planes."

"My father supported me completely, and when I was old enough, and though it cost him dearly, he sent me to that very airport for training. I spent years learning all there was to learn about flying those marvellous machines as well as all the mechanics that went into making them work. They were the happiest days of my life."

"It was while I was there that I met Rachael." He noticed the questioning look on my face. "Yes, the same Rachael that you saw on the night we escaped. I fell in love with her. We were married and within a year, a daughter was born to us—a daughter who bore a striking resemblance to her mother, and who possessed her mother's unique trait that very few women had."

A thought struck me and, briefly, I wondered if that daughter could be me. But then I realised with a pang that that daughter would be about seventy years old by now. I sighed.

"We were never able to have any more children," Jack continued. "Though Rachael would have dearly loved it, and all our love was lavished on our only child. She grew to be as beautiful as her mother, married and, in turn, had a daughter of her own. This daughter, my granddaughter, was so bright and so beautiful that even strangers noticed her. Needless to say, she attracted attention wherever she went, even as a small child."

Jack sighed. "Then came the war."

"We had been watching the armies of the enemy mow down everything in the countries across the ocean from us, but we never thought they would reach us." For a moment, his hand doubled into a fist and he thumped his knee with it. Then he relaxed, spreading his fingers out against his leg. "But they did," he went on, hoarsely.

He cleared his throat. "Suddenly, it was our turn. Every able-bodied person was called into the service in some capacity."

"We fought long and hard," he said. "But, in the end…well, you know what happened in the end." Jack looked away again, but not before I caught the shine of tears in his eyes. "I had been captured," he continued, finally. "But I managed to escape and after a long and often perilous trek, was able to make it back to my home city—or what had been my home city. Everything was gone. The city had been levelled. Not one building stood." I saw his chest heave as he struggled to control his emotions. Finally, he continued. "There were scattered groups of refugees who lived by what they could find in the rubble, and from them I was able to get enough information to start tracking my family."

"Rachael and our daughter had decided to share an apartment when our son-in-law and I had gone into service, so when the city fell, they had been taken prisoner, and had gone together." He looked again at me, misery swimming in his eyes. "It took almost a year, and, at times I didn't have much of a trail to follow, but I finally reached the camp where they had been taken. Rachael was still there, and our daughter, but our ten-year-old granddaughter had been sold to a farmer some distance away. We never did find out what happened to our son-in-law."

He scrubbed at his eyes with the back of a weathered hand. "I cannot describe to you how I felt when I finally crept into the camp and held Rachael and my daughter in my arms again, only to be told that our little granddaughter would not be coming away with us when we made our escape. Something in my heart seemed to break and die."

He paused for a moment, then took a deep breath. "But somehow you keep on going, and we did. Escape was remarkably easy. I took Rachael and our daughter to a village that was safe and protected, then I went in search of my littlest girl."

He paused. "I never did get to the farm where she had been taken. I was captured only a few miles from there, and I spent the next thirty years serving under various masters, doing whatever jobs they assigned me, but never forgetting my family for an instant."

"They must have known that I was one who would try to escape because they never stopped their vigilance. But I could never quit thinking of my family in all that time. I had no idea what had happened to any of them, but I kept living day to day and continually looked for an opportunity to flee. The years slipped by and I lost hope of ever seeing any of my loved ones alive again."

"Then came the call for an aeroplane mechanic, at the very farm where my little granddaughter had last been living. My background as a pilot was unearthed and I was chosen."

"Imagine my feelings when almost the first worker I saw was my own beloved Rachael—thirty years older, as I was, but just as beautiful to me." He grimaced. "We had to be very careful. Obviously no one knew of our relationship, and we could not give a hint of our emotions to anyone. By working slowly and carefully, we were able to snatch brief minutes together without anyone growing suspicious and I was able to find out what had been happening in her life since I had been gone."

"The village where they had been living was one of the last to fall and the villagers who survived were scattered. Rachael had been taken captive, but…but in the fighting, our daughter was killed. We wept together as we shared this grief, even though many years had passed between. Then I told her how I had tracked our granddaughter to the very farm where we were before I had been captured."

"Rachael wept anew at this news, for she wondered if it could have been possible that her own granddaughter had been living so close for so long. There had been one young woman of whom she had heard. She had possessed great beauty and the same peculiar feature that Rachael, herself possessed. She had wondered at the time, but had decided that the coincidence was too great. She had put it out of her mind. The young woman had delivered and been marked and then, after a few years, she was gone."

"All Rachael could discover was that she had been too outspoken and that she had been sold. Later, she overheard a conversation between Master and one of his friends about Master's peculiar young one being the only one of her line left and Rachael figured that it meant that the mother had died. Whenever she was on duty in the museum, Rachael would take every opportunity to look down into the farm to see if she could catch a glimpse of this particular child, though she must have been an adult by this time. But the distance was too great and there were always many workers milling about so she could never be sure."

Suddenly, Jack's eyes were on me. "Liss, the peculiar trait that Rachael possessed and passed to her daughter and granddaughter was her bright, beautiful red hair. We believed this young-one that we heard about—certainly you were the only one at Master's with flaming red hair!—was *our* young-one." He smiled. "We were not completely certain until we saw you, but you look so much like your mother—like your grandmother, herself—that…" he paused, obviously trying to control his emotions.

I touched my hand to my head. What was he saying? Surely he couldn't believe…!

Jack reached out and took my hand. "Liss," he said softly. "We think that you are our great-granddaughter. We are offering you our love. It is all we have left anymore, but there is plenty. Liss, don't leave us."

The tears were flowing quietly down his leathery cheeks now and he pulled a couple of scraps of material from his pocket and used one to try to wipe them away. The second, he handed to me. Only then did I realise that my blurred vision was due to my own streaming eyes and I now held the cloth to my face and sobbed aloud into its folds.

When I had finally regained my composure, I turned to him. "Grandfather," I said and threw myself into his arms, sobbing anew at the knowledge that I belonged to someone. Not with papers of ownership, but with ties of the heart and blood. Full understanding came slowly to me and his story became more and more my own as I thought about it. No more were the people in his past mere acquaintances. They were mine. I belonged to them. I felt for the first time as if I were a person, as real as a master. I felt as if I had grown several inches in those few moments.

Then suddenly I remembered the woman I had seen so long ago in the garden at Master's. It was then that I knew I had been watching my mother.

"I saw her," I whispered between sobs as the awful reality of everything burst upon me. "I saw her on the last day that she lived at Master's. I saw them take her away. I saw it all." I looked down. "I am sorry," I said, "I didn't know."

What I could have done if I *had* known was unclear, but suddenly, I was grieving for the woman who had stood in that garden in her filthy clothes and defied the world.

Jack's arms tightened about me and his body shook with his silent sobs as he shared my distress. We sat there for some time grieving quietly and too filled with emotion to move or speak.

Finally, I collected my self.

"But what of Rachael?" I asked, pulling myself out of his arms and suddenly remembering the sweet, grey-haired woman who had helped us to escape and who had suddenly become so much more than our helper to me. "Were you planning to go back for Rachael?"

"I was and I am," he said decisively. "I have been planning her rescue since we flew out of the canyon. I think one of the hardest things I have ever done was to leave her behind."

"But why did she not come with us when we made our escape?" I asked, looking up into his face.

"She would not," he said simply. "She wanted to be sure that you were taken safely away, and she felt that she could help best by doing all in her power to stop or at least slow down any attempts by the masters to find or follow us. She is waiting for me to return for her. Our plans are set, and daily she watches for my signal." He turned to me, a question in his eyes.

I thought of the masters. Of what they had done to me and my family. But I knew what I had to do. "Yes, I will be going, too," I answered the unspoken words. He sighed heavily and started to rise. I placed my hand on his arm. "You must understand me," I said urgently. "I am going with you to bring back Rachael, and Meg and her baby."

"And you?" he asked, his face becoming hopeful.

I looked away for a moment, thinking. Finally, "I will not stay there," I decided. "But you must promise that you will help me bring Young Master back here."

His mouth opened to retort, but I spoke quickly, "We can kidnap him if possible, but he must come and see this place. Perhaps he will want to stay. We have to try. Jack, it is my only chance at happiness."

"I know we will probably regret this," he said, tiredly, "but I can deny you nothing. We will bring him back if we must tie and gag him to do it. But promise me that I may release him if he will not learn and accept our ways."

"I cannot promise that," I said. "Well, yes, I guess I can, if you will release me, too."

He sighed. "Done," he said. He offered his hand.

CHAPTER EIGHTEEN

Our preparations were not extensive, but did require the work of the next several days.

Jack left me to myself and, aside from looking over my few belongings to decide which I would need, I had little to prepare. I continued to spend time in the library, and indeed, learned many things even in that short space, but my heart was no longer with my books and I soon tired of reading—spending less and less of each day with the dusty tomes.

My life was taking an exciting turn and the upcoming events occupied my thoughts to the exclusion of all else.

I did spend some time with Ross and Mia, trying to explain my position to them. At first they refused to believe that any reason could induce anyone to return to the slavery at Master's. I was surprised at Ross' choice of words, but I realised that what he said was true. Nevertheless, I continued to try to make them understand and, as I explained my feelings for Young Master, I struck a sensitive note and they looked at each other and nodded. I might not have their full support, but at least they understood my feelings.

The people of the village could only guess at what life was like at Master's and similar places, but they were dismayed that we were going back, even for a short time. I spent many hours trying to explain my position to Rebecca and then Ramannah, but neither of them could understand my single-minded attachment to one man. Surely, they thought, I could find someone here in the village that I would come to love as much. All I had to give it was a little time.

But I knew what I had to do and preparations continued for our trip.

Finally the day that Jack had chosen arrived and he and half of the village stopped at my door in the hour just before dawn. I had never convinced any of them that I was doing the right thing, so it was a silent and subdued group that met me. I had packed a small sack with things I thought I might need, and Jack reached for it, looking solemnly at me as he did so.

I answered the unspoken question, "Yes, Jack, I have to go."

He switched my bag into his left hand and reached for my hand with his right. Then we started off towards the barns, and the village fell silently into step behind us.

The early morning air was soft and cool, the sky was a luminous blue, with just a hint of green towards the eastern horizon. There were a few wisps of cloud here and there, but it was mostly clear. Jack looked up and sniffed appreciatively. "Ahh! Just smell that air," he said. "Perfect flying weather." I knew that he was trying to sound cheerful and I appreciated his effort. But I gripped his hand just a little tighter at his words.

I had flown, but it was still a new and rather terrifying experience to me. In the two months since we had come here, I had been able to understand much more of what had happened to us during our escape, and with knowledge had come fear. I could now understand the danger involved.

Jack's plane was standing quite close to the eastern wall just beyond the village barns. It had been pulled almost under a grove of apple trees. I started to move towards it, but I realised that Jack was going to walk right past. He kept on a straight course and I looked at him questioningly as he took a firmer grip on my hand and towed me along behind him.

"We are not using the plane," he said, without looking at me. "We don't have enough fuel for the trip." I thought of the great distance to be travelled. In the plane, it had taken eight or nine hours. On foot, we could not hope to complete the journey in less than a month.

We walked on, our feet making little sound in the long, soft grasses. Finally, we reached a portion of the village fields that I had not before seen. The eastern wall made a sudden jog outward, leaving an extra grassy area almost the size of the village itself. Here, in the small box-like canyon, a huge balloon floated.

It was the colour of the sky on a sunny day, blue and luminous and fully as high as five huts if stood one upon the other. Many ropes had been thrown over and around it to harness and control it. Indeed, it needed control. Already, it seemed to tug and jerk at its tethers, wanting to be free.

We walked closer and I saw that a large basket, half the size of the inside of my cabin, had been fastened to its underside. One of the men of the village stood inside the basket directly below the balloon, and I saw a tongue of flame leap up beside him, accompanied by a roaring sound.

Here, then was one of the hot-air balloons that I had seen pictures of. I wished suddenly that I had taken the time to read a little about them because there could only be one reason for this one's presence now.

Jack intended for us to travel in it. Already, he was throwing my bag of necessities into the basket and turning to help me up.

A ladder made of twined ropes hung over the side and I clambered in easily and glanced around for somewhere to sit. There wasn't a stool or chair in sight, so I squatted quickly on the floor of the basket. Jack climbed in behind me and dropped lightly onto the tightly—woven floor beside me.

He nodded at the man who had been standing in the basket, and the man smiled and clambered out.

Rebecca came close and for a moment, I thought she was going to come with us, but she handed me a large sack and stepped back.

Then one of the village elders approached us, his eyes on Jack.

Jack nodded at him, folded his hands together and bent his head.

Everyone else did the same.

The elder began to pray. "Dear Father, bless them," he said. "Their journey will be long and dangerous. Please keep them safe and return them, in joy and success, to us. Amen."

The assembled group repeated the word and I was surprised to hear an answering response from my own lips. For the first time, I, too, petitioned this unseen, unknown 'God'.

I knew that Jack and I would definitely need His help.

Jack lifted his head and waved his hands in the air, and two of the men untied the heavy ropes that held us anchored to the ground.

Slowly we began to lift.

I shut my eyes tightly and felt as though I were sinking instead of rising. Thinking something had gone wrong, I quickly opened them again and stood up, supporting myself by grasping tightly to the side of the basket. But no, we were rising, amid many calls of "safe journey!"

Our trip had begun, and only the God we had all prayed to could know how it would turn out.

It did not take long for the upturned faces to become a blur and then to fade entirely from sight. We seemed to be going straight up and I wondered just how far we would rise before we ran right out of air or drifted off. But soon I realised that we were indeed moving forward and that all our progress was not in one direction.

Once we had risen above the walls of the valley, I could see that we were travelling in a south-easterly direction and for the time being, the mountains rose parallel to us on either side and were not threatening. Jack was busy checking the equipment that was firmly strapped to the center of the basket directly below the balloon. I walked, shakily, over to him and sat down nearby where I could get a good look at what he was doing but would not be in the way.

The machine looked a little like a stove, but it had a huge nozzle on the top, which opened out directly below the balloon. I knew that this contraption must heat the air that kept us afloat, and I was fascinated by it.

Jack was tapping the cover on a small gauge set into the shining steel side of the stove. Directly below this gauge near the floor of the basket, a four-inch hole had been punctured in the heavy covering. A small canister was inserted into this hole, almost disappearing completely inside the stove. As I watched, Jack grasped the canister with a special tool and twisted it to the left. With a slight hiss, it came free. He pulled it back and handed it to me. I expected it to be hot, but it was not and I held it easily.

At one end, the container tapered in to form a nozzle and it looked like a small, fat bottle. There was no printing on the side, and it was painted a plain, bright red, but I figured it must have contained a very concentrated fuel, and was, perhaps, one of the most important pieces of equipment on this trip.

Jack picked up a bottle identical to the one I held from a familiar-looking case near him. Moving over to it on my hands and knees, I realised that it was one of several such cases that had been packed in the plane on our trip out.

Looking back at Jack, I saw that he had now fastened the tool he carried onto the lower half of the bottle in his other hand. Then he pushed it into the small hole and twisted it to the right.

Again, I heard the hiss, and the needle in the gauge suddenly flipped over to the other side. Jack sat back and wiped his hands on his robe.

Rising, he pushed the case of canisters over to the side of the basket and strapped it there. Then he reached for the bottle I still held and placed it in another, empty case, also strapped to the wall.

Moving back to the stove, he pulled upon a lever. I was startled to see a bright lick of flame leap upward toward the balloon, accompanied by the loud roaring sound I had heard before. I expected to see the whole cloth contraption above us suddenly catch fire and dissolve, but instead, I felt it lift, the force almost sending me to my knees.

Jack looked at me, "Sorry about that Liss," he said, smiling. "It has been a while. It'll take some time to make it move a little more smoothly."

I smiled shakily back at him. The idea of travelling at a height of several hundred feet still made me uneasy and though the take-off in a balloon was a little less frightening than in a plane, we were still a good deal higher than standing on a regular kitchen stool. And that was as high as I wanted to be.

The next hour was a test of Jack's admittedly long-unused skill as we wove around the mountains. The perfect weather helped, for we could clearly see where we wanted to go and could avoid problems before they became problems. Jack was concentrating on controlling the balloon, or as he put it, "finding the right air currents in the tricky area", so conversation was limited and I was free to look about me.

Even in the plane, the view had not been so spectacular.

Now, in the early morning sunlight, the mountains seemed to float on a sea of rose-colored mist. Their forests were a deep emerald-green, and I caught sight of several waterfalls that had escaped my notice on our last trip. Everything appeared new and fresh and I took a deep breath of the marvellous air.

One of the mountains was very close and we passed so near to it that I could almost touch the tips of the trees. As it fell behind, I turned to make a comment to Jack. My words froze on my lips as I saw that he was sweating profusely and mopping at his brow with the sleeve of his robe. He looked at me, "That was a close one, Liss," he said, and I realised that I had been enjoying a sight that might well have spelled our ruin.

How little I knew, even now.

We moved around the next towers of rock, and I could see that these were much smaller in size than those we had already passed, and suddenly we were out of the mountains. Looking down, I saw that we were once again over the rolling hills. Time seemed to crawl by but finally I noticed that the hills were levelling out and we were once more over the familiar plains.

Without anything to mark our passage, we seemed to be moving very slowly, and I watched as our shadow slipped silently across the smooth plains below us. Suddenly I caught movement out of the corner of my eye, and I turned and saw a herd of animals streaking across the ground. I pointed them out to Jack and he turned his head.

"Those are antelope, Liss," he said, surprise in his voice. "They used to roam in huge herds all along this area. I thought they had been killed off entirely during the war, like most everything else, but I guess I was wrong. Some of them must have reached a safe place and remained there until the grass returned to these plains. Their presence is a good sign that our poor old land is recovering. It's been a long, long time."

Jack continued to lean over the edge of the basket and watch the small herd until they were mere dots behind us. It was then that I realised that though those animals had been running as hard as they could, we had easily outdistanced them.

"We are moving fairly fast, are we not?" I said to Jack.

"Yes," he said, his eyes still on the spot where he had last seen the antelope. He sighed and looked at me. Tears sparkled in his eyes and I knew that his thoughts had been back in the Before Times, when he had been young and great herds of antelope had roamed freely. He pulled a cloth from a pocket and dried his eyes. "Yes," he said again. "You don't seem to move at all in one of these contraptions, but they really do 'cover the ground' if you'll pardon my pun."

I smiled in answer, not really understanding, and turned my attention back to the countryside slipping past us.

Throughout the morning, Jack stayed beside the stove and pulled on the lever to regulate our height. At times he let us drift quite close to the ground and I was able to get a good look at the deep scars and crevices that were mute evidence of the Great War and its devastation. There were also huge patches of bare soil, even yet, and I knew, from my books, that these were the sterilised areas created by the above-ground explosions that had caused such deadly havoc.

I was encouraged though, by the sight of green grass and plants growing next to these areas, as though the land was slowly being reclaimed and healed.

As the sun rose higher in the sky, I was suddenly reminded that I had not taken time for breakfast. I moved carefully over to the small heap of sacks and stored items and picked up the bag that Rebecca had handed to me. Opening it, I found that it was full of food and soon Jack and I were munching on sliced meats sandwiched between thick pieces of bread and several varieties of raw vegetables. A bottle of cool milk and several early apples finished off the meal.

Brushing crumbs from his lap, Jack again rose to stand beside the all-important lever. "We're going to have to find a new stream of air," he announced presently. "This one is pushing us a little too much to the south."

I stood up beside him. "Will that be difficult?"

"Oh, no. Just a matter of rising or dropping and finding the right one." Even as he spoke, he pulled upon the lever and sent us up several feet. Waiting a few seconds, he repeated the manoeuvre and suddenly I felt a push from the west that almost sent me sprawling.

"Hang on," Jack said, grinning. "This is a strong one. It isn't going exactly in the direction we want, but still it will gain us several hours. I think I'll ride it for a while."

After a few minutes, I decided that I was used to the increased movement and I stumbled over to him. "You must be getting tired," I said. "Teach me how to run the lever."

He looked at me and smiled, "Always out to learn something new, aren't you, Liss?" he said. "Very well, come here and I'll show you. All it takes is a steady hand and a cool head."

He placed my hand on the lever and waited. Soon I could feel the basket begin to drop beneath us. Using steady pressure, he pushed down on my hand and the lever. The roar startled me and the blast of heat almost made me pull my hand away, but soon I felt the balloon lift again and he removed his hand. The heat stopped.

"There, that's all there is too it," he said. "Just feel with your feet and knees and spine what the balloon is doing. Once you know how to correct it, doing the correcting is very simple." He stood there beside me, swaying as I worked the lever a little too quickly, but always explaining and encouraging.

Before long, my corrections were smoother and I needed less instruction. Finally, he sat down on the floor beside me and I knew that he had enough confidence in me to relax for a while.

I continued to work the lever for the next several hours and we travelled directly east for much of that time. Jack finally stood up and stretched from his cramped position. He knelt down and checked the gauge, then rose and walked over to the case of canisters. Reaching in, he pulled out a fresh bottle and proceeded to exchange it for the one in the stove, which must have been almost out of fuel. Stowing the used one neatly away, he came to stand beside me. The afternoon was warm, the sky cloudless, and the land silent.

"I always love it up here," he said, his eyes on the horizon. "It is so peaceful."

I smiled at him, careful not to let my attention wander from my job.

"Liss," he said suddenly. "Has Young Master ever given you any hint that he cares for you?"

I was surprised at his question and found it hard to answer for a few seconds. "No, I don't think so," I said slowly. "We never really exchanged anything more than glances. I used to catch his eye a lot, but I thought it was because I had such a bad reputation for listening in where I should not, that he was just keeping watch over me. It doesn't matter to me, though."

"It will," he said solemnly. "It will matter more to you than anything else in the world. Even more than living." He reached out and gave my arm a squeeze. "The reason I ask such a question is because of what happened on the night we left," he said. He was silent for a few seconds. Then he looked at me. "Young Master was at one of the windows of the house and saw us escape."

I looked at Jack, sucking in my breath sharply. Even one of the bombs that had turned the Before Times into the present could not have startled me as much as Jack's statement.

"I know that you saw him too, Liss," he went on, "He did nothing. He could have easily raised the alarm, we would never have outdistanced him or anyone he chose to call, but he did nothing. I have often wondered about that."

"Losing four good slaves would be quite a financial blow," he continued. "The only thing I could think of was that he wanted us to escape. But why? He could have wanted Ross to leave, or even Mia, or me. But none of us was in any way remarkable or facing any major changes in the near future. On the other hand, you were. His father had just begun to notice you and the time for your carrying was coming very close. I had overheard them talking about it on one occasion."

I pursed my lips thoughtfully. I did not tell Jack that I must have listened intently to the same conversation. "And they seemed to be opposed as to what they should do with you, though Young Master had no concrete ideas."

"Yes it all seems to come back to you," he said thoughtfully. "I think Young Master is in love with you, though he probably would never admit it and maybe doesn't know it himself."

My eyes were wide with shock as I listened to his reasoning. It couldn't be true. I needed to think this through. I left the lever and walked over to the side of the basket, sinking slowly to the floor.

I looked up at Jack. He had his hand on the lever but was watching me. As he caught my eye, he nodded firmly and turned his attention back to the countryside. I lay back and tried to make sense of what he had said. It was no use. It just made me sleepy. Before long, I was unconscious of everything around me as I drifted away by myself.

Much later, I awoke to find that the sun had set and that the balloon was losing altitude. Thinking something was wrong, I scrambled to my feet and looked around. Jack had stacked two boxes together and was sitting on them, still maintaining his position near the lever. As I watched, he rose to his feet and pulled upon a cord, which disappeared up into the balloon itself, still keeping a careful watch over the side of the basket as he did so.

Following his gaze, I saw that we were sinking into a large canyon, enclosed much the same as the one in which the plane had been displayed. For a moment, I thought that we had arrived and that this was the canyon next to the museum. But as I looked around, I could see that there were no settlements nearby. The plains stretched wide and empty around us. I looked at Jack.

"We have to stop for the night," he said quietly. "We both need to rest and we still have quite a way to go. We will arrive sometime tomorrow."

Even as he spoke, I could see the ground coming up at us. "Too fast!" I thought in panic and crouched down into the basket.

We thumped heavily into the soft earth and for a moment were pulled almost over onto one side. But the basket righted itself and we were sitting once more on solid earth.

Jack flipped a switch on the stove and I could see that when the heat was cut off, the balloon slowly deflated and drifted over to the side. Jack scrambled out and grabbed for it, laying it out carefully along the ground.

Once the fabric was smoothed out, it looked enormous, stretching across half of the field upon which we sat.

Jack signalled for me to come and I climbed out of the basket and walked stiffly over to him. My legs felt as though they were still in the air, but I managed to reach him without falling over.

Together we folded the yards of material neatly, careful to keep the ropes which surrounded them straight and untangled, and left them in a pile beside the basket.

Then we began to unload necessary items and set up camp. Jack scooped dirt to make a depression in the ground, then had me find any sticks or wood that I could in order to build a fire.

I wandered around in the waning light and finally stumbled over a patch of scrub brush and stunted trees in a hollow. There was plenty of old, dried wood and I soon had a large armful. Jack built up a fire while I went back for several more armloads of wood. Then we ate with the warm light of the flames flickering across our faces.

As soon as we had finished and tidied up the camp, we rolled up in blankets near the friendly blaze and, in spite of the rest we had each had earlier in the day, were soon asleep.

It seemed as though I had hardly closed my eyes before Jack was shaking me awake. "C'mon, Liss. Time to get going," he said, softly.

I groaned and turned over on my back. The sun was still below the horizon, but the whole eastern sky was a glorious shade of pink. For a moment, the brilliant colour made me think of the village and suddenly I was swept by a wave of longing to see everyone and be in my own cabin again. I brought myself back to the present.

I knew that sunrise was not far off. I stretched and pushed the blankets off my legs, then looked for the boots that I had set beside my bed the night before.

My robe had climbed almost to my knees as I slept and I stood to let it drop down where it belonged. I was trying to smooth out the wrinkles when Jack returned and handed me a package.

"These might be a little more convenient for what we have to do today," he said.

I opened the parcel and discovered a uniform, much like that which I wore as a worker, but of a black material. "You change in the basket," Jack said, "I'll change here."

I quickly gathered up my boots and walked over to the basket. Throwing my boots and uniform inside, I climbed in after them, and changed as quickly as I could. I was struggling to tie my boots when Jack called out to me.

Standing, I saw that the sun had risen and that Jack was spreading out the huge bag of fabric, readying it to receive its fill of warmed air.

I clambered out of the basket again and helped him spread out the folds of cloth.

Jack grasped the hoop that formed the bottom of the huge bag and began to swing it in strange swoops before him. I could see that air was literally being swallowed by the balloon and before long, his actions had lifted the limp sides almost a foot.

He continued to force air into the bag for some time, then finally satisfied, he pulled the end of the balloon into the basket. I climbed in after him and held it while he lit the stove. Carefully he held the bottom of the bag over the nozzle at the top of the stove and allowed the newly warmed air to flow into the balloon.

As the bag filled and the danger of igniting it had gone, Jack began to use the lever. His efforts caused the balloon to rise higher and higher until, as before, it was tugging at the basket, ready to be off. Jack had tied a length of rope to a stake pounded deeply into the ground, and we tilted crazily as it held us down.

Finally, pulling a knife from its sheath, Jack hacked at the rope as far down as he could reach. It parted and we were free.

The sky was clear and blue above. Hardly a cloud appeared to mar the view. Below us, the morning sun shone on a plain that was completely covered with thick, lush grass.

Jack nodded towards it. "That proves that we are getting closer to the settlements," he said uneasily, and sure enough, within a few hours, we were passing over the small farms and towns that belonged to the masters.

Jack tried to keep from using the lever when we were near these settlements. The balloon by itself could slip by unnoticed, but the roar of the flame would certainly attract the attention of anyone who heard it. I looked down into those places and made out small figures of workers in fields and gardens. I could not tell if they could see us, and could only hope that they did not.

Towards noon, I noticed that Jack was watching the land very intently. Occasionally, he would reach into a pocket of his robe and pull out a small thick disk.

I moved over to him and looked into his hand, realising as I did so that it was a compass that he carried and that he was trying to figure out our exact location.

He spent some time in making the balloon lift and lower, looking for just the right current of air. Finally, he consulted his compass and nodded his head. "We're almost there, Liss," he said. "Just another hour or so in this direction and at this speed and we will be able to set down and prepare for tonight."

"Are we to wait for darkness, then?"

"Yes, our chances will be much better with the cover of night, even with the light colour of our balloon," he said. "Once we have landed, I will tell you my plan."

Even as he spoke, I could see that we were approaching yet another farm. I wondered how he would be able to set this great balloon down anywhere and remain unseen. It seemed impossible.

Within a short time, however, I saw a great patch of bare earth straight ahead of us. It seemed to cover miles. As we moved closer, I could see that at its center, the earth had been broken up

171

and huge pieces had been torn out and lay crumbling on the surface.

Jack allowed the balloon to lower until we were directly over this area. As we crossed mountains of broken earth, I scanned the ground for some possible place to set down. Jack pointed directly ahead and I strained to see beyond the tangle of debris.

Soon, it seemed as though the earth dropped off into nothingness, and as we came closer, I could see that it was one more of the great canyons, brought into being by the huge bombs.

Smoothly, Jack guided us over this opening in the ground and let the balloon settle down inside.

Our landing this time was slower and I hardly felt the basket hit the soft sand in the canyon bottom.

Jack immediately shut off the stove and jumped out of the basket.

I smiled as I followed him. Jack was almost ninety, yet from the back, he could be mistaken for a man much younger and he was certainly active for someone his age.

Together we carefully folded the blue cloth and again tucked it down beside the basket. Then we stood and stretched and looked around. All was quiet.

"There was a good deal of action in this place during the war," Jack said. "It was the halfway point between two great cities. The conquering army had taken possession of the one city and was ready to wage their own brand of war on the other. But the other city proved mightier than they had expected. The men of that city brought the fight to them and away from their own wives and children.

"The men held the armies off for months. Their final surrender heralded the end of the war. Everyone, including the conquerors, were tired of the fight. Maybe if the men of that great city had known at the time how close they were to defeating those armies, they might have held out for just a few weeks longer. But they didn't and with them, we all fell."

I turned slowly and surveyed the canyon. The ground in the bottom of it was very broken, certainly we had landed in the smoothest section. Below us to the south was a wide river. It looked as though the great opening we sat in had been blasted out of the side of a cliff and was really just an inward extension of the cliff face now.

I looked down at the quiet water flowing past us. Had it looked the same when men were fighting for their survival on its banks all those years ago? The sight of it calmed my troubled thoughts somehow, and filled me with peace. I smiled to myself as I turned to begin unloading the basket.

"We will not take out anything but what we need for preparing our lunch and dinner," Jack said to me as I approached. "We must be ready to leave and we need to rest until then." I nodded my head and reached for the sack of food. It was getting lighter and I wondered how we would feed everyone on the trip back.

If our mission was successful.

Jack and I ate a simple meal and cleared away all that we had used. Then we crawled into the basket and spent the next few hours trying to sleep. The night ahead as well as the following days would probably be hectic, and we needed to get our rest now.

Surprisingly, we did sleep, because suddenly the sun was gone and night was fast approaching.

I sat up and stretched. Then I stood and looked around for Jack. He was standing beside the river, looking down into the quietly flowing water. I called to him and he turned and beckoned to me. I jumped to the ground and joined him at the water's edge.

"The night is still and perfect, Liss," he said quietly. "Come, sit down and I will tell you my plan, such as it is." We squatted there by river and I watched in fascination as the light of a sliver of moon was reflected on the slowly moving surface.

Jack cleared his throat and I looked up at him. "The plan is very simple," he said. "The only problem is that we have so much ground to cover in a short time. We will try to land the balloon on the far side of the museum. There will be less chance of being noticed there. Rachael knows my code on the door, so we will go to her first. She can help us reach the others."

"You probably know the growing buildings better than anyone, so we will send you for the baby. Once you have it, you must travel around the north side of Master's property and the canyon where we got the plane. The baby will be most unpredictable, perhaps crying out. You must get away from the buildings as quickly as possible and stay outside of the compound."

"I am going to fetch Meg from the Stable and the two of us will be able to lure Young Master out of his house. That is the only part of the plan that scares me. If he puts up a fight, I will have to try to subdue him. It has been a long time since I have had to do anything like that."

He rubbed one hand over his eyes, then looked at her. "I hate it."

He sighed. "Transporting him will be difficult too, if I have to resort to violence. I can carry him for a short distance, but I'm not sure for how long. Our job would be much easier if we didn't have to take him." He looked at me, but I slowly shook my head. He sighed again. "There won't be a heavy guard posted, I'm sure, in spite of the fact that there has been a recent escape from Master's property."

"And that's it. As I said, my plan is not complicated. I have found in the past that the simplest plans are the ones that work. They allow for problems that arise. Do you have any questions?" Again I shook my head. "Then let's go."

We spread out the huge sheet of cloth and went through the same steps we had followed only this morning. In a short time, the balloon was full and impatient to be off. I clambered into the basket behind Jack and wished that I could pray, as the villagers were so fond of doing.

I felt that we needed someone's help on this dark night.

Jack pulled the lever and I sawed at the rope that bound us to the earth. The basket began to tilt as the rope held us down from one side. Finally, the fibres parted and we started to rise. The night we had prepared and travelled for was finally here.

We were off.

The ride was uneventful. The land looked different in the darkness, lit only slightly by the light of the portion of moon overhead. Everything seemed to be covered with a silver sheen, making it look almost…unreal.

We flew over Master's farm and the museum as Jack searched for the right landing spot; tried to manoeuvre the balloon through the unpredictable night currents. Fortunately, we were able to refrain from using the lever, the only tangible sign of our presence in the darkness, while the settlement was directly under us.

It seemed odd to be looking down at the place where I had lived my whole life. It was the same, and yet it seemed to be so different. I was looking at it with the eyes of knowledge now, and no longer as one of Master's programmed slaves.

We sank toward the ground and I knew that Jack did not dare to use the lever so close to the buildings. We just barely slid over the museum, and actually scraped some of the very tallest trees on the other side, as we searched for a landing.

Once beyond them, we found a wide clear spot and Jack let us sink to the ground once more. The landing was rough, but I was too excited to notice.

We were almost there. Surely we would succeed.

CHAPTER NINETEEN

As soon as we touched ground, Jack was out of the basket and grabbing for ropes to secure us to the trees which formed a dark curtain to the east of us. When the sounds made by our landing had died down, we waited quietly for a few minutes to see if any alarm had been risen. We heard nothing. Even the woods between us and the museum were silent.

Jack changed the bottle of fuel for a fresh one and turned a dial on the stove. "I sure hope this works, Liss," he said. "I'm trying to keep enough warm air rising above the heater to keep the balloon inflated and afloat. Our take-off may have to be hurried."

I knew what he meant. If we were followed, we may have to outrun Master's people.

When he was sure that the basket was secure, Jack reached inside and pulled out a bundle. This, he strapped onto his back. Then taking my hand, he turned toward the museum.

We walked the length of the building, and I could see that he was once again making his way towards the great front doors. We stayed within the cover of the trees as much as we could and tried to make little noise.

Finally, we found ourselves in the same grove that had received us only two months before. We squatted there and waited.

Jack turned to me. "The door is open," he whispered.

I narrowed my eyes, trying to pierce in the darkness. At first, all I could see was the great black entrance. Then I realised that what he had said was right. One of the doors was swung wide, and there was a figure standing in the doorway. A figure dressed in light-coloured clothes.

We strained to see clearly, and I suddenly noticed that the figure was getting larger.

Then I realised that whoever it was had left the doorway and was making slow progress towards our hiding spot.

I half turned, ready to flee, when Jack gripped my arm. Wait!" he whispered urgently.

I sank back down once again and watched the figure approach.

It moved close to the trees and stopped. I heard a quiet voice, "Jack, is that you?"

"It's Rachael," Jack breathed, standing and moving towards her.

I followed closely, keeping a handful of his uniform in my hand. Here, then was my great-grandmother. How different it was to see her now, having learned so much about her.

Jack embraced her and I could see the tears glisten on his cheeks as he stood back and looked at her, cupping her face tenderly in his hands. I was sure that she was crying also, but it was difficult to see her face because her back was to the meagre light.

She turned slightly and I could feel her eyes surveying me. "Does she know?" she asked Jack, keeping her eyes on me. "Have you told her?"

"Yes, she knows," Jack answered, turning also to me.

Rachael moved towards me and reached out with both arms. "Oh, my darling girl," she said, her voice breaking. "We've waited so long for you." She wrapped her arms around me and leaned her grey head against mine.

I was suddenly enveloped in a sweet scent that I had never smelled before. It was at once pleasant and somehow comforting. Of their own accord, my arms went around her frail frame and I squeezed her tight.

"Whoof!" she exclaimed, laughing softly. "Someone has been keeping you strong and healthy!"

I smiled at her and I could hear Jack chuckle. "I've waited a long time for you, too, great-grandmother," I said and could feel tears pricking my own eyes.

We gave each other another squeeze and then she turned back to Jack.

"I heard the sound of your approach and knew that you had used the balloon as you said you would," she said. "But we must leave quickly. Others may have heard also, though few would recognise the sound if they did. Still they would investigate. Everyone is tense and there is much trouble brewing. Patrols pass by every few hours and checks are performed at random. There have been threats, supposedly from a neighbouring farmer, and they say that he will fight Master for what should be his."

Rachael shrugged her slender shoulders. "I have taken no notice of this feud apart from when it concerns me or the other workers, but it has been noticeably escalating. The other night, two of Master's workers were found shot dead in one of Master's fields. This neighbouring farmer is being blamed for it, though I have my own opinion as to who is responsible, and I have heard that Master is ready to fight."

"Who?" I asked, my voice squeaking in excitement. I cleared my throat and spoke more slowly, "Who was shot?"

"I know only that they were part of the farm crew and that they were both men," she said. "Master has moved all of the children and his whole family away from here."

I could feel the blood thumping in my ears. Suddenly I knew the fear that my great-grandparents and so many millions of others had known during and after the war. Part of her words penetrated.

"Family? *All* of his family?" I repeated stupidly, "And the children?" I was crushed by a sudden wave of despair. I turned to Jack, "Then how can we do what we came to do?"

Rachael looked at me, startled. She reached out and gripped my sleeve. "What did you come to do?" she asked.

Jack grasped her shoulders again and turned her towards him. "We wanted to take Meg and her baby with us," he said. He looked at me, then back at Rachael and added, "And Young Master."

"What!" Her voice was almost a shriek and she visibly controlled herself before she spoke again. "A master? Why? Isn't that what we are trying to leave behind?"

"Rachael, try to understand…" Jack began, but Rachael would have no part of it.

"We can't possibly risk everything for a master!" she hissed at him. "Look at what they have already done to us. Do you want that to continue? Do you?"

"Rachael, please," Jack tried again.

"No!" she cried, grasping the folds of material at Jack's chest. "We can't even think of it. We have to…"

"I love him," I said quietly.

Rachael let her hands fall to her sides and she turned back to me. "What did you say, Liss?" she asked.

"I love him," I repeated, looking at Jack for encouragement. "I have loved him for a very long time. I just didn't know it until I learned enough to understand what I was feeling. I have to be with him."

"But it's impossible," she said, tears starting in her eyes again. "It's so impossible." The spark had burned out as quickly as it had flamed, and her voice was dull and lifeless.

"We have to try," said Jack, quietly. "We were going to at least try."

Rachael's shoulders sagged, but she nodded and turned back toward the museum doors. "I understand," she said quietly. She sighed. "Young Master stayed behind while his father took the rest of the family to safety. He is down there now, trying to keep everything calm."

We followed her almost to the door of the museum, when she suddenly straightened and turned towards us. "Did you say Meg and her baby?" she asked.

"Yes," Jack said in surprise. "Why, what is the matter? I suppose that the baby was moved with all the other children, wasn't it?"

"But Meg hasn't had her baby, yet," Rachael said. "They just took her to the hospital this morning. They always give the women two days to settle before the operation is performed. I was expecting it to happen late tomorrow or early the next day."

"That is a bit of luck!" Jack exclaimed. "We must have had our dates wrong! Perhaps we can accomplish what we came to do after all. Now all we have to do is get Meg from the hospital and bring her back here, if she can walk that far. Liss, you will have to do that and I'll have Rachael help me. First, though, Rachael, I need you to change into this."

Reaching into the pack that he had taken from his back, Jack pulled out some folds of dark cloth. I recognised another uniform similar to the ones which Jack and I wore. Rachael took it and disappeared silently into the museum. We retreated to the shelter of the trees and waited. Soon she was back, a dark shadow flitting silently across the ground.

Jack turned to me. "Your job will be much simpler, now," he said. "All you have to do is go to the hospital and find Meg. Bring her back to the balloon and wait for us there. If the balloon is deflated, try to get some air back into it, as quietly as possible. If we get there first, we'll do the same. Anyway, we'll meet you there!" Jack and Rachael each gave me a quick hug, and the two of them melted into the shadows.

I was on my own.

As quietly as I could, I made my way back along the east side of the museum. Below me, I could see Master's house gleaming white in the darkness. Beyond it, I could make out a little of the compound. Everything was quiet.

Suddenly, I saw a group of figures dart from the shadows surrounding the offices. They ran as far as the Stable and then disappeared into the blackness which covered it. Only a few seconds after they had disappeared, I saw an orange flash that filled the offices with light. Then a dull boom reached me and I realised that someone had just set off an explosion in the building. The windows burst outward and flame followed them, licking immediately up the wooden sides of the structure.

As I watched, one side slowly caved in, groaning as it did so and the flames shot into the night sky. From directly below me, a siren began to grind, and suddenly there were people everywhere. I could hear a small popping sound and for a few minutes, I could not understand what it was.

Then I saw a man dressed in a light-coloured robe start across the compound on the run. Halfway across, there were several pops and he fell and didn't move. It was then I realised that, for the second time in my life, I was hearing the terrifying sound of guns.

Who was shooting at whom, I could not tell, but the sound shocked me into activity and I forgot caution as I raced down toward the inert figure. Several persons had materialised out of the shadows and were standing around the body when I reached it, most of them workers I recognised.

I was surprised to see that they were holding guns.

Something stirred at the back of my mind for an instant, but when I tried to examine it, it was gone.

Shrugging, I forgot about it.

I pushed through the crowd, ignoring their startled comments and knelt beside the fallen man, for man it was, and, by his robes, a master, too. Slowly, I turned him over, and breathed a silent sigh of relief when the face proved to be one that I had never seen before. He was quite dead. I stood up, and someone touched my shoulder.

"Liss, when did you get here? Where have you been?"

With a start, I realised that everyone was looking at me. No one was interested in the dead man, or at all concerned by what had just happened. I wondered briefly what had been going on here since I left. I shook my head, pushed through the crowd and started at a run towards the hospital, slipping into the shadows of the slope on the north side of Master's house.

Glancing back, I could see that several of the workers had started after me, but suddenly, the air was split by the sound of another explosion, this one from one of the outbuildings near the office, and the workers scattered. Briefly, I hoped that Jack and Rachael would be able to complete their end of the mission.

I continued with mine.

The hospital was on the far north end of Master's property, beside the growing buildings. It lay mostly in darkness, though there was light streaming from some of the windows on the south and east, and I was easily able to keep to the shadows as I approached. The doors stood open and people were milling around and pointing at the fires on the other side of the compound. I took advantage of the confusion and managed to slip—hopefully unseen—into a small door, which opened just to the left of the main doors.

I was in a small dimly lit corridor. Three doors opened off of it, all swung wide. Moving silently, I peered in each doorway. The rooms were dark, but I could make out the shape of pallets inside, smoothly made. The rooms were empty.

I moved back into the corridor and headed toward the door at the other end, reaching for the knob.

As I did so, I suddenly realised someone was on the other side, fumbling with it. I dove into the last room on the right and pressed myself against the wall behind the door. I looked wildly about for something to use as a weapon, but all I could see was the neatly made bed. I stopped breathing. I could feel my heart shaking my body, and I felt prickly all over as beads of moisture dampened my skin.

At least two people had entered the corridor and I could hear their voices as they came into this portion of the building. "Is everyone accounted for?" It was a male voice speaking.

"Yes, Master," a female voice answered. "All the patients have been moved to the kitchen area at the back of the building and are being guarded there. There are only three right now. A female and two males."

"Have they been here all night?" the male voice asked.

"Oh, I'm sure they have," the female answered. "The one male is recovering from a broken leg, and the other from a horse kick. The female is here for delivery and marking."

"Good. Keep an eye on them." The voices had continued down the length of the corridor and I now heard the outside door open and close.

Carefully, I peeked out, pulling back as I saw the female standing at the door leading outside. She fumbled with it and I guessed that she was securing it. Then she retraced her steps. The inner door shut behind her with a click and I immediately slipped into the hallway and reached for the knob.

Relief filled me as it turned easily and I realised that she hadn't locked it. I pushed the door open a crack. It opened into a bisecting hallway.

The woman was just beyond the door, her back to me. She was bent over and seemed to be studying something on a desk, against the wall in front of her. Then she straightened and turned to the right, disappearing down this new corridor.

I pushed the door a little wider and looked to the right and left.

The woman turned a corner down the hall and disappeared. The long bright passage now stretched empty in both directions.

I breathed a long sigh and looked around. Beside the desk, almost directly across the hall from me, I could see another door. Figuring that the back of the hospital, the kitchen, must lie in this direction, I softly moved into the corridor, closing the door behind me. I crept quickly across to this new door and tried the knob.

It, too, turned easily and I found myself looking at shelves of dishes and kitchen utensils. A storage room. I moved inside and pushed the door shut.

A large rack of knives hung in front of me and without knowing why I did so, I reached up and took down the longest one, hefting the weight of it in my hand. Feeling a little more secure, I started to search for a second exit.

I soon discovered it as I skirted a tall set of shelves. It was on the opposite wall and I moved carefully forward. Reaching it, I pressed my ear close to the cold metal, straining to catch any sound.

I could hear the murmur of voices and knew that someone was in there. I grasped the door handle and gently turned it. It moved silently and I pushed the door open a crack. Inside, was a brightly-lighted kitchen, all gleaming silver and white. For a moment I was taken aback at the wonder of it and I could not help but compare it to the equipment Meg and the people of the village had used to prepare meals. The differences were staggering.

Sudden movement along the far wall attracted my attention, and I saw three people, two men and one woman seated quietly on stools. All of them looked unutterably weary, and one of the men actually had his eyes shut and had propped himself against the wall. The other man was studying the floor, but the woman was alert and I could see her looking about the room.

I watched her gaze move down the wall next to me and across the door which shielded me. Suddenly her eyes met mine and I saw them widen. My heart leapt as I recognised Meg. She rose slowly to her feet, her body heavy with her baby. Suddenly, a door beside her opened and a man poked his head in.

She hesitated and then turned to him. "I cannot sit here any longer," she said firmly. "I must lie down in my room. I could not possibly cause any trouble in my state and my only wish is to rest."

The guard stood there for a moment and finally nodded his head, coming into the room and closing the door behind him. He walked toward the door behind which I crouched, and in a panic, I pushed it shut and looked frantically for a hiding spot.

A shadow was cast across part of the room by a shelf filled with dishes, and I shrank back into this meagre shelter.

I had only just hidden myself when the door opened and the guard ushered Meg through it. Then he led the way across the room and through the doorway into the corridor.

As quickly as I dared, I followed, opening the door a crack and peering into the hall behind them.

The guard simply moved down the hall and opened the next door opposite.

He allowed Meg to walk past him into the room beyond, then closed the door and went back up the hall. Even before his footsteps died away, I was across the hall and opening the door to Meg's room.

She was standing directly behind it, waiting for me. "Liss, I never thought to see you again!" she said, with warmth in her voice. "Why have you come back? Did you set off that terrible explosion?"

I shook my head. "No," I told her. "We have come for you . . . and your baby."

Meg's hand went to her swollen belly and she stroked it gently. "My…baby?" she repeated, softly. She again looked at me, "Is Jack with you?"

"Yes, and we must hurry. We have a conveyance on the far side of the museum, tied to the trees. I have to get you out of here and over to it."

She nodded her head and grabbed a blanket off of her bed. I frowned as I noted its light colour, but it couldn't be helped and I threw it about Meg's shoulders.

185

Opening the door a crack, I looked down the corridor. It remained deserted. Perhaps everyone was outside watching the fires on the far side of the property.

We swiftly moved through Meg's doorway and the one through which I had come and we were in the small corridor. Moving quietly, we reached the far door.

Kneeling down, I tried to see the lock in the dim light. I soon realised that it was not a lock but a simple bolt and I only needed to slide it back. I did so and we cautiously swung the door open.

There was still a group of people clustered around the corner of the building, but their attention was all for the fires in the other direction, so we crept out and made our way carefully to the west.

Within a few tense seconds, we were around the corner and out of their sight.

We hadn't been noticed.

As quickly as we could, we moved around the compound, then up the hill to the museum, keeping to the shadows as much as we could.

Once in the deeper shadows which blanketed the walls of the museum, we made good progress until we reached the far end.

Meg was breathing quite hard by this time, and I sat her down on the ground with her back to the cool stone wall of the museum so she could catch her breath.

Then I turned and looked once more into the compound below.

Lights were on in every building, and Master's house was lighted from the top to the bottom. The scene would have been beautiful, except for the blaze in the east. The fire had nearly consumed the office by this time, and the small outbuilding had been reduced to glowing embers.

A group of people stood in a line beside the pump at the Stable and passed buckets of water from hand to hand, pouring them on the blaze. The office was far beyond saving. The concern now seemed to be to keep the fire from spreading.

I tensed suddenly as I saw another group of shadows appear from around the west wall of the Stable and move swiftly toward the line of workers.

Several members of the bucket brigade fell as the onslaught hit them, and the rest fled in every direction. The sounds of the clash reached me seconds later and I could hear shrieking and yelling and the popping sound that was gunfire. I searched the area for Jack and Rachael, but I could not tell who anyone was.

I turned to Meg.

"Follow me!" I said over my shoulder as I ran toward the place where we had left the balloon. I turned one last time as I entered the woods.

Meg was following slowly, staying in the shadows. She would make it.

I ran as fast as I dared through the woods and finally saw the basket of the balloon through the trees. I waited just for a moment within the line of growth, then I ran over to the balloon.

No one was there.

"Jack!" I called softly. No answer. They hadn't made it yet.

I turned and raced back through the trees. Halfway, I met Meg. "They aren't there yet," I panted. "You must make your way by yourself! I have to see what has happened to Jack...and everyone."

"What?" she asked, confused.

"Go and wait for us," I gave her a little push, indicating the way. "Just look for the strangest contraption you have ever seen, a giant bubble with a huge basket attached. It is there, in the trees." Again, I pointed. "You'll know you're there when you get there." I started to run. "I will explain later!" I shouted over my shoulder.

I skidded to a halt at the top of the slope. The lights had been lit in the museum and poured out of the windows, casting pools of light on the dark ground. I quickly scanned the compound below.

There were groups of people struggling together all over Master's property. I could see bright flashes of light as more shots were fired and the sounds reached me a fleeting instant later. Somewhere down there were Jack and Rachael…and Young Master.

I started down the slope, and it was then that I realised that I still clutched the knife I had found in the hospital. I took a firmer grip on it and continued down. I slid a little on the grass, which covered the hill and skidded out of control down the steep slope.

My forward impetus was halted abruptly as I ran headlong into an immovable object at the base of the hill. The wall of Master's house. Dazed, I sat down hard on the ground. I waited there a few moments until my head cleared and I could once more take a normal breath.

Then I stood up cautiously and looked around. On this side of the house, all I could see were its imposing bulk and the patches of light that escaped its windows and fell to the ground. The sounds of the battle were louder and clearer here, however.

I sidled along the house, poking my head above several of the windowsills. The rooms were empty of people. Finally, I was able to peer around the corner. A group of people was running towards the steps at the front of the house and I ducked my head back as the night air was filled with the pounding of boots hitting the wooden stairs. I shrank back further as the sounds of shattering glass and breaking wood reached me.

The group moved into the house, but all was silent except for the noise made by their trail of destruction.

Finally, I heard angry shouts and cursing. The men had encountered no one. It was then that I remembered that Master had moved his family out. And I knew also that Young Master was not inside.

I skirted the house and started carefully down the second slope toward the main compound. I could see several groups locked in a deadly struggle as I approached, but who the individuals were, I could not tell. All I could make out were the robes of masters and the uniforms of workers. Faces were indistinct, though I crept as close as I dared to several of them.

But somehow, even as I peered through the eerie, flame-shot darkness, I knew that none of them was Young Master.

I kept to the shadows when I could and reached the Stable without incident, though I had to step around several groaning or horribly still people to do so. I checked each person that I passed carefully, and breathed more easily as I recognised none of them. I was sorry to pass by those who needed help, but there was no time to stop.

I shrank against the side of the building as a man came skidding around the corner. He raced right past me and I was surprised to recognise one of the men who had often called on Master when I had lived here.

Immediately behind him and running just as hard came one of Ross' men, his face frozen in a mask of hate and anger. This worker carried a knife that equalled my own in size and I could only guess and shudder at the fate of the man he chased, if he ever caught up with him. I moved away from the wall of the Stable and began to edge cautiously toward the south side.

From just around the corner, I could hear the sounds of yet another struggle, and I stiffened and felt a wave of fear wash over me, in spite of what I had already seen.

Then I heard someone call, jubilantly, "We've got him!" There were a few grunts and the sound of blows, and Harry and one of his workers came around the corner, half-carrying a man between them by draping his arms over their shoulders.

He was dressed in a black robe and his head hung down limply, but I knew who it was even before Harry saw me and called again, "We've got him!"

He grabbed a handful of the prisoner's hair and lifted the limp head to reveal Young Master's perfect features.

CHAPTER TWENTY

For just a moment I felt frozen, as if everything in me had suddenly stopped. Then my mind began to function again, the thoughts coming so quickly that I could hardly grasp them. I knew that I would have to act fast, before they brought the rest of the workers.

"Leave him here with me and get us something to carry him in," I commanded. "There must be a wheelbarrow or something in one of the storage buildings still standing. Go and get it quickly. We can use him to buy our freedom. Go! Quickly!"

The two men dropped Young Master to the ground and the other worker was off like a shot, but Harry was a little more suspicious.

"Who are you?" he asked quietly. I moved into a shaft of light. "Liss!" he exclaimed in surprise. "How...When...?"

"I have come to help the rest of you to escape!" I said urgently. I could almost taste the lie on my lips and it was bitter indeed. These people had been my co-workers, my friends. But Young Master's life came first and I could not endanger him.

He stirred slightly and I could see that his eyes had opened. Harry was not looking at him, however. His eyes were on me.

"Where have you been, Liss?" he asked softly, moving towards me. There was a strange light in his eyes and suddenly, I was remembering Rodney from so many years ago. I felt the fear go through me and I backed slowly away, circling around toward the wall of the Stable as he advanced. "Did you escape and become a free person?" he asked. "What is it like to be a free person? You can tell me. It is Harry, remember me? I had...feelings for you."

He was still moving slowly forward and he kept his eyes fastened on mine.

My heart was beating wildly and I recognised terror in its rhythm. I continued to back away.

Suddenly, I remembered the long knife I held. Gripping it with two shaking hands, I raised it and pointed it at him in what I hoped was a threatening gesture.

Harry ignored it, keeping his eyes locked with mine.

I continued to retreat, finally feeling the rough, immovable wall of the Stable against my back.

Harry stepped over Young Master's still form and followed.

Suddenly he paused for a moment and I almost lowered my meagre weapon. Then he stretched his mouth, showing yellowed teeth in a hideous caricature of a smile, and lunged at me, his arms outstretched. I thought to be imprisoned by his arms, but instead, he collided heavily with me, knocking me sideways and we both fell to the ground.

The knife was wrenched from my hands and I scrambled to one side and regained my feet, expecting at any minute for him to do the same. But he lay where he had fallen.

I saw movement just beyond him and I almost screamed. I clapped one hand over my mouth as I recognised Young Master, slowly getting to his feet and I realised that it was his action that had saved me.

He had tripped Harry and sent him into my knife. We looked at each other for a long moment.

Then another explosion filled the air and we both jumped, realising once more the danger of our position.

We shrank back into the shadows and I reached out and nudged Harry with the toe of my boot. He did not stir.

I looked at Young Master. "Is he…?"

"He's dead," he said quietly. "Liss?" I looked up at him, trying to read his expression in the darkness. "Why did you come back?" I could feel the cold suspicion that dripped from the words.

Before I could think of a reply, he surprised the breath from me by pressing me against the wall of the Stable with one arm. Several workers charged past and I realised that he was once more protecting me. He withdrew just as quickly after they had passed and my arm and shoulder tingled where he had touched.

I opened and closed my mouth several times, not sure of what to tell him now that the opportunity was here. Finally the words came. "I returned for you."

His eyes flared and he clenched his hands tightly as they hung at his side. "For me?" The suspicion died in his voice. "But I am a master, one of the hated race."

"I do not hate you." I said simply.

Suddenly, Harry's worker charged around the corner, pushing one of the farm wheelbarrows. He stopped beside Harry's still form and looked around. He did not see us there in the shadows and knelt, grasping Harry by the shoulders and rolling him over. He reached for the limp arms and started to drag the body toward the cart.

When the meagre light struck the lifeless face, the worker stopped as though he had been struck. He stooped and peered closely at Harry, reaching out to touch the handle of the knife, which protruded from Harry's chest and was now plainly visible. A muffled exclamation escaped him and he rose suddenly, looking wildly about.

Someone ran past the west end of the stables, shouting as they went, and the worker turned and, in panic, sprinted off in the direction from which he had come, leaving his cart and the still body behind.

Young Master grabbed my arm and began to hurry me toward the slope south of his house. "We must get out of here," he whispered urgently. "It is getting far too dangerous…" he looked back at Harry, "…for either of us."

We crept from shadow to shadow, standing motionless when someone tore past, and crouching close to the ground when shots rang out, but finally, we gained the comparative safety of the slope and scrambled quickly upward.

Once at the top, we stopped just inside the first of the trees and looked back down into the compound. When I had caught my breath, I turned to him. "Young Master, what has been going on here?"

He moved slowly over to a fallen tree and sat down. "My Father and I made a strategic error," he said. "We did not tell the workers that you and the others had escaped. Rather we let them think that you had been sold."

I looked at him in surprise as I sank down beside him.

"Yes, I know it was a stupid idea, but we thought that others would try the same thing if they knew that you had gotten away."

"There were those who knew the truth, however," he went on, "and the word soon trickled through the ranks. The reaction was worse than any of us imagined. The workers went berserk. They broke into the storage houses and found our stash of weapons, such as they were. I sent a distress signal and received a reply, but reinforcements did not arrive until a short time ago, and when they did, they were met by a group of armed and very angry and determined workers."

"Father had already left with my mother and sisters and all of the young ones, so I had been trying to keep a handle on things." I glanced at his dark robes. "Yes," he said, smiling a lop-sided smile. "I was on guard duty, for all the good it did. But at least I wasn't in the house when your friends came to call."

I shuddered at the thought and looked down at the house, still brightly lighted from top to bottom. The damage done by the angry workers was not visible from here, and it still looked peaceful and serene.

Young Master picked up a stick and jabbed suddenly and violently at the ground with it. The suddenness of his movement startled me and for a moment I was poised to flee, but I looked at his face and relaxed again. His eyes told me that he meant me no harm.

"All along, we have suspected our nearest neighbour, a man named Ryley, of trying to overthrow my Father and seize his council position and our lands," he said. "It was only recently that all the trouble seemed to point at someone within our own settlement. I think I knew for sure on the night that two of our workers were killed. The crime was so cold-blooded that I knew that Ryley was not behind it. Whatever he may be, he is not a killer."

Something again stirred in my memory, but this time, I was able to catch hold of it. I was once more back in my office on the day that I left Master's. Master and Young Master were just outside my window, discussing their concerns about a neighbour named Ryley. Young Master had suspected then that the persons responsible had come from inside the compound walls. I suddenly knew that it had been workers who had planned and carried out the break-in. That they had been trying to start trouble between the two Masters even then.

Something didn't fit, however. If they had planned and carried out the disturbance in the office, were they also responsible for the murder of two of their fellow workers? I couldn't believe what my logic was telling me. "But how could the workers have killed two of their own people?" I asked Young Master. "It just doesn't make sense."

"It does if you realise that they were trying their best to frame someone else and perhaps cause such feelings that the two Masters declared war on each other," he said. "During that eventual clash, the workers must have thought they could take over, or that they could make their escape. They just went too far. That is what makes this whole thing so sickening. They would even kill their own if it would further their cause. The moment I was sure who was behind all the unrest was the moment I also realised that we had accomplished nothing in all our years of thinking we were superior and could force our *superior* ways on everyone else."

He looked at me and I was surprised to see that a tear was making slow progress down his cheek. "We tried to eliminate the humanity in our workers and something terrible happened," he said softly.

"We succeeded."

He looked down. "We will pay the price for generations!" His voice trailed off into silence and he sat there with head bowed. The crushing weight of what he and his people had done seemed to rest upon his shoulders.

I could taste the despair.

Suddenly, it was hard to breathe. I felt an overwhelming need to put my arms around him and hold him, but my courage failed me. In an effort to escape this pain, I forced myself to stand and look past him into the compound. There were two or three more fires burning now, and I could see the hospital was alight and slowly being consumed. Movement near Master's house distracted me. A group was moving towards it, carrying torches, and I watched in awful fascination as they climbed the steps and went inside. Then I saw the light of flames leap up in the top floor windows and I looked quickly away.

Young Master had risen to his feet and was also watching the destruction of his home. "Come with me," I said, touching his shoulder. He stood for a long moment, and then he finally nodded his head and turned and followed me through the woods. He walked heavily and I could feel the sadness and weariness that stalked every step.

Soon I could see movement through the trees, and I stepped out and into the arms of Jack and Rachael. They were quite tearful in their welcome, but Jack took my hand and looked into my face. "Liss, we just couldn't find him," he said gently. "There was too much confusion. We barely escaped with our lives and we dare not go back. We will have to continue on. There isn't anything more we can do. You do understand that, don't you?"

I smiled at him and patted his lined cheek. "I don't have to," I said, turning to look towards the trees.

Their eyes followed mine and I heard them gasp as Young Master stepped out of the shadows.

Meg was seated with her back against the basket and she, too, was startled.

I spoke up quickly, breathlessly, "I've brought him. They would have killed him."

Jack moved toward Young Master, and the latter stiffened, unsure of his reception. "You understand that we are leaving here?" Jack asked. "That we will never return."

Young Master looked at me, then back at Jack. "I understand."

"Do you want to come with us? I know that it looks like you have very little choice and I'm afraid that Liss is quite insistent, but I want your assurance that you will cause no trouble."

Young Master looked steadily at him, and then he again looked at me. "Liss is insistent?" he asked softly.

"It was one of the reasons that we made this trip," Jack said. "She was unsure of your feelings for her, but she was willing to take the risk."

"I will come with you," he said.

"You know that you will be our equal," Jack pressed. "That we will work side by side?"

"I'll come with you," Young Master said again.

"I can't call you Young Master," Jack said, grimacing.

"My name is Adam."

"Welcome, Adam," Jack said, reaching forward with his right hand. Young Master…Adam, gripped it and I could see Rachael and Meg relax.

"Tell me what you need me to do," Adam said. He helped us as we spent the next minutes getting ready to leave.

Jack's experiment had been quite successful, and the heat rising from the stove had kept the balloon almost fully inflated.

We needed only to climb aboard and use the lever for the final lift.

Once everyone was inside, Jack pulled upon the lever and the resulting roar seemed to echo for miles in the stillness. He pulled again and again, and finally we could feel the basket start to lift.

Something fluttered down beside me and drifted to the ground.

Startled, I looked around and saw that Adam was once again dressed in his white master's robe. He looked at me.

"No more sneaking around," he said.

I nodded.

As we floated up into the dark sky, I could see the torches moving up the hill toward the museum. Below us, Master's house was a tower of flames as orange tongues shot out of the windows and greedily began on the roof. Other fires were burning brightly and the whole area was quite light.

I prayed to the God of the villagers for those who were left behind. I hoped that they, too would find peace after this night of horror.

CHAPTER TWENTY-ONE

The trip back was long and plagued by problems. It was cramped in the tiny basket and we could not travel for any great length of time because of Meg's condition. The added lift required for the extra people also used up our precious store of fuel canisters. We had little food left, and on two occasions we were forced to hunt wild animals to eat.

Meg especially felt the lack of food and in addition, was totally frustrated at her very limited ability to help with even the simplest chores. She asked for nothing and was always ready to encourage and offer advice when she saw the need, but she could not think of this as helping in any concrete fashion, and the time weighed heavily on her hands.

Despite the difficult aspects of the trip—I was often hungry, having given my portion of food to Meg—I can remember only my feelings of happiness. At times, I felt as though I was going to burst. I was surrounded by the people that I cared most for in the world, and I knew that they shared my feelings.

We were again floating over a herd of antelope. Adam and I were standing together, leaning on the side of the basket and watching the animals streak across the grassy plain.

Suddenly, Adam touched my chin and turned my face towards him. "Liss, I have something to ask you," he said sombrely.

I lifted my eyebrows in mute question.

He looked down and fidgeted with the tie on his robe for a moment. Then he looked once more at me. "Do you love me?" he asked.

I stared at him.

"Liss, I really have to know," he said. "Is that the real reason you came back? Because you love me?"

It was my turn to look down nervously.

Finally he again reached over and turned my head towards him.

I looked up into those clear brown eyes. "Yes, Adam, I do," I whispered softly

For a moment, his eyes flared with some emotion I was unsure of. Then he took a deep breath and smiled. He reached out and let one long finger slide down my cheekbone to my chin. "I have loved you for so long," he said quietly. "Since the first moment I saw you, when you 'became' an adult." He looked away and shrugged, his face twisting into a grimace.

"I didn't know what to do about it. There wasn't anyone I could talk to. I lived in a constant fever, afraid I would have to explain my thoughts and actions to Father or another master who happened to notice my...interest."

"Things finally reached a climax when Father told me that it was time for your first visit to the hospital. I couldn't bear it. May Heaven forgive me, I hadn't given it much thought when the other female workers served their time at the hospital. But not you. Never you. I decided then that I had to get you away. I simply couldn't stand the thought of you bearing any other child but...mine."

He turned to me once more. "I couldn't understand my feelings at first. We were taught that workers were not human but merely possessions, like horses or cattle."

I turned to stare at him accusingly.

"We were taught that, but I never quite agreed with it!" he defended himself. "Affection between a master and worker was accepted as long as it was the same as that found between a man and his dog or cat. Any stronger emotion could only be looked upon as...a perversion."

Through his halting words, I sensed some of the struggle that he had faced, for he had been taught his role as strictly as I had been taught mine. His feelings had bewildered him, threatened to jeopardise his future and would have cost me my life, for no worker could be allowed to live who inspired such forbidden feelings in a master.

Adam had spent months trying to figure a way to sneak me out of the compound. It was he who had found the plane and balloon and had arranged for their purchase by the museum. He had toyed with the idea of restoring them and then taking me away himself, using one or the other, but his knowledge of either was limited, and he was more than grateful when Jack was found and solved those problems for him.

Later, he heard about Jack's plans for me and realised that Jack was going to solve his entire dilemma. He would never tell me how he had discovered this, but I suspected that it must have been a worker loyal to him who had overheard Rachael and Jack.

Adam had felt mostly relief when he had seen us on the night we escaped, though part of him had despaired that he would ever see me again.

"I saw you," I said. "Watching us as we went around the house towards the museum. I couldn't figure out why you didn't raise the alarm."

"I couldn't do that when Jack was accomplishing the exact thing I had been racking my brain to accomplish!" he said. "The only thing that mattered was your safety." He looked down once more, his eyes absently following the herd below them. His voice lowered, hardly above a whisper. "I was willing to give you up and never see you again if that would mean you were safe."

His hands had curled into fists and he thumped them against the rail of the basket.

I uncurled the long fingers and slipped my hand into his. "And that is exactly what I was trying to do for you," I said. "Get you away and keep you safe."

He smiled at me.

I shuddered to think of what our lives could have been like, had we remained at Master's, and I was so grateful that, this time, he chose to come with us. After this, there would be no going back.

We had been travelling for three days, and were becoming exceedingly weary of the trip when, in the middle of the afternoon, Jack pulled the cord which allowed air to escape from the balloon, allowing it to sink downwards in preparation to land. I looked over at him questioningly, but he was watching the ground. He was very careful of his landings because of Meg and this time was no different. We touched down lightly.

I looked over at Rachael to see if she knew why we were stopping, but she was squatted down in front of Meg. From where I was sitting, I could not see Meg's face, so I rose to my feet and made my way over to her. As I reached her side, I could see that she had both hands on her belly and a very strange expression on her face.

Adam had placed a foot on the rail of the basket and jumped as soon as he had felt the balloon touch down, and now he was running to secure us by driving stakes into the ground and wrapping the anchoring ropes around them. Jack smiled at him and I knew that he was grateful for the help of a younger, more agile man.

Meg and Rachael stood up stiffly and moved over to the side also. Jack placed a box filled with empty canisters and helped Meg to stand on it. Adam had returned and he reached for her from the outside of the basket and helped her to slip over and onto the solid ground. Then he did the same for Rachael and me. I smiled as Adam reached for me, remembering the number of times that I scrambled in and out of the basket on my own. But it felt good to have his arms around me and I stayed close to him for a few seconds, feeling his arms tighten briefly before he set me down.

Jack had hopped out and was laying out blankets for Meg to stretch out on. I walked over. "When did the pains start, Meg?" he asked as he helped her to lie down.

"Only a few minutes ago," she answered, sighing as she relaxed into the soft makeshift bed. "There has only been the one. Perhaps it is not time yet and they will stop."

"According to your dates, your baby is due in two days," said Jack, as he reached for the container of water that Rachael brought over. He poured Meg a drink and he and Rachael sat down beside her.

"Yes. I was surprised when they told me that they were ready to perform my delivery because according to the Healer, I had seven days to go. Then they said it was normal procedure to take the baby, or as they put it, to do my *delivery and marking*, one or even two weeks early." Meg's voice slowly dwindled away and she bit her lip and closed her eyes. Jack was watching her intently and Rachael moved close and placed her worn hand on Meg's swollen belly. After a few moments, Meg again opened her eyes and let out a careful breath. Then she smiled at us. "Do you think it is the real thing?" she asked.

"The pains are not very hard yet," Rachael said gently. "If it is the onset of labour, it is only the very early stages. Hopefully, we will know within the next hour. Either they will intensify, or they will stop."

Meg laid her head back on the blankets and closed her eyes. I saw Rachael and Jack exchange a look. Then they both rose and walked over near where Adam was laying the balloon out across the ground.

I followed them.

"What will we do?" Rachael asked. "We cannot deliver her baby here, in the middle of nowhere."

"We could, if we had to," said Jack. "We've both had the training. Oh, I know it was a long time ago," he said as Rachael opened her mouth. "But it not easy training to forget." He sighed.

"Still, I'd just rather get her to the village if I can. We must be pretty close by now - we are almost into the foothills. It will be a lot more pleasant for everyone if we have the clean surroundings that we can only have in a cabin."

"I guess you're right," Rachael said at last. "We could do it, if we had to, but a cabin would be better." She sighed, "I've tried to prepare her for what is coming, to explain what has happened to her body and what will continue to happen, but in our talks, I always assumed that everything would happen in the village with many experts to help. I have not prepared her for a birth on a blanket in the middle of the prairie."

"A birth is a birth," said Jack, putting an arm around Rachael's shoulders. "It will really make little difference to Meg where she is, as long as she is comfortable. My only worry is for the baby in these conditions."

"Will the baby die?" I spoke up.

"Certainly not!" said Rachael indignantly. Then, realising that it was I who had asked, she took a deep breath, then spoke more calmly. "Liss, we are only concerned for the *comfort* of the baby and the mother. Certainly these are not ideal circumstances, but births have occurred under many strange and often much worse conditions."

I glanced over at Meg. "Can I help in any way?"

"We'll let you know if the need arises," Jack said gently.

Adam finished tending the balloon and came over and joined us. Then we walked back to Meg and made ourselves as comfortable as possible. We waited for several minutes and Meg fell asleep.

"Is she going to have her young one now?" Adam whispered to me

"We are not sure yet," I answered him. "Do you know much about it?"

"I can remember the birth of my two younger sisters," he said. "I picked up a lot of what was being said and done at that time."

I smiled at him, then turned to see Rachael lay a gentle hand on Meg's face.

"Sleep is a good sign," she whispered. "If her body can stay relaxed, maybe the pains will stop."

"Or maybe that will bring them on," Jack interrupted, smiling as Rachael made a face at him. "We'll just have to wait and see."

An hour or so later, Meg awoke and sat up. She appeared rested and refreshed. She smiled at everyone's anxious faces and patted her belly. "We must have had a little sleep," she said.

Jack smiled, "You've been out for over an hour," he said. "How do you feel?"

"Much better," Meg said. "I think things have settled down for a while. Let's get home while we can."

No one needed to be urged. We helped Meg into the basket and Jack and Adam proceeded to get us off the ground. It was not very long before we were once again airborne. Jack walked over to the case of canisters and reached for one. As he did so, I noticed that there was only one left. We were running out of time in more ways than one. Jack exchanged the bottles and stowed the used one.

Then he turned the lever over to Adam and walked to the side of the basket. He peered over for a few minutes and then looked closely at the mountains on the horizon. "I think we're almost there!" he said excitedly. Rachael joined him at the rail and he put his arm about her narrow shoulders. I could imagine what they were thinking.

I joined Adam beside the stove. "How do you feel?" I asked him.

"I think you could best describe my feelings as scared," he said.

"But these people would never harm you," I said. "They will accept you as they did us."

"It is not fear for personal safety that I am concerned about," Adam said softly. I had to bend quite close to catch the words. "I am concerned about how I am going to treat you."

"Me? What have I got to do with it?" I asked in bewilderment.

"I'm afraid that I won't be able to live as a real person," he said, looking down. "I'm worried that I will be cruel without even knowing that I am. I was raised by a different set of laws than you. I was raised to rule and that will be difficult to forget. I will probably be autocratic and insufferable and very, very difficult to live with." He paused, then looked at me. "Liss." I looked up at him. "Do you think you will be able to handle it?"

I looked fully into those deep brown eyes that meant so much to me and said, "I've been called pretty strong in my lifetime. I think I can handle it."

He put an arm about my shoulders. How natural these gestures of affection were becoming for both of us. Still keeping a careful hold upon the lever, he pulled me close against his side. In companionable silence, we watched the landscape go by. The mountains, which were once again a dark wall on the horizon, were growing larger and closer with each passing second.

Soon the land below us began to roll gently, thrusting a little higher and a little higher as we drifted past. I watched the play of expressions on Adam's face as we approached the first of the mountains. Jack once more took control of the lever and made a careful passage between the giant formations.

I now knew the danger that each mountain represented and I could not enjoy the view as I had in other trips through here. I held my breath as each tree-coated mountainside loomed closer, and relaxed only after it had fallen behind us, only to tense again as it was replaced by yet another. Even so, the formations were spectacular as they rose up on all sides of us, and I could see that Adam and the others were spellbound.

We wove in and out for long, tense minutes, which stretched into a long, tense hour before we broke through the last of the mountains and saw again the plain with the long seam running through it.

Jack shouted, "We're home!" and everyone burst into shouts of joy.

We had come out of the mountains just a little to the north of the village and had to travel south for a way to find it. The people in the village must have been watching for us because several large, bright balloons suddenly floated up out of the canyon.

I couldn't keep the smile from my face and, looking around, I could see that the happiness was contagious.

Jack manoeuvred us carefully between the walls of the canyon, his aged hand steady on the ropes and levers. He cautioned Meg to sit down, which she did, but his words of caution fell on deaf ears for the rest of us. We were standing, watching the upturned faces as they grew nearer, even, to Jack's horror, leaning over the sides in our excitement.

The balloon finally touched down gently and Rachael helped Meg to her feet. The people crowded around us, calling and cheering. The noise was deafening. Then Adam put a foot on the rail and leaped lightly to the ground, dragging the anchor rope with him.

The crowd gasped and were instantly silent. I saw parents grab for their little ones. Men push families behind them. Everyone shrank away from us. At first I wondered what had alarmed them. Then I saw their eyes fastened on Adam's robe.

Adam's *white* robe.

Though stained and dirty, it was still very recognizable as a hated and feared *master's* uniform.

Adam froze, uncertainty replacing the welcoming smile that had been on his face.

I leaped from the basket and moved quickly to Adam. I could hear someone following me, but I didn't bother to turn to see who it was. My eyes were only for Adam. And the fear I could feel coming from him.

I put my arms around him and held him closely. Then I turned to the crowd. They were watching us carefully. I smiled and took Adam's hand, making a show of twining my fingers through his. The crowd seemed to relax, though they still regarded Adam with suspicion.

I caught a glimpse of Isaac on the outer edge of the crowd. He, too was watching Adam's tall figure, but I had a harder time defining his expression. Anger? Pain? It was indeed curious. I dismissed him in favour of a more pressing need—introducing my beloved Adam to our 'family'.

Ramannah came forward. Stately, regal, she stopped before Adam and looked down at him. Studied him carefully. I hid a smile at Adam's expression. I don't suppose he had experienced looking *up* at very many people!

"You are a master?" she asked finally in her careful English, putting one hand on his shoulder.

Adam looked at me, and at my eager nod, turned back to Ramannah. "I *was*," he said softly, emphasizing the word. "I am not now."

Ramannah nodded and, keeping one hand on Adam's shoulder, turned to the people. "Our family is once more complete," she said, still in my language. "Let us celebrate the return of our brothers and sisters!"

A loud cheer erupted from the crowd and they surged towards us. For a moment, Adam's eyes widened and he pulled me back beside him, thrusting one arm around my shoulders. Then we were surrounded by smiling faces and he realized that, whatever their customs, these people did not mean us any harm.

Meg was lifted in strong arms, carried to my cabin and made comfortable in Mia's old bed. Then the whole village erupted in a celebration our successful return.

I saw several of the young village girls look appreciatively at Adam, but I was very happy to see that he had eyes for no one but me. The girls, too seemed to realise that he was mine, and they drifted back to their own friends.

The young men of the village took Adam's arms and led him to one of the cabins on the male side of the village. He was soon back and I covered my mouth with my hand to hide my smile as I looked at his new green robes. No more was he a master.

Now he too, was free.

EPILOGUE

Meg's baby was born a week after we arrived, a strong, healthy boy. Motherhood is strange for her, because she has never had or seen a mother, and instinct only covers the basics of a baby's care. But she had watched over all of us in the Stable and she uses those protective feelings now to build upon.

Rachael helps a good deal, and her gentle instructions come from a heart aching to love again. Now it is a common sight to see Rachael and Meg seated side by side in the village square, talking quietly while Meg's baby suckles, wrapped snugly in a blanket.

Often Mia joins them. She and Ross have a baby growing, due sometime in the spring and she is busy with tiny robes and diapers and learning all she can from Meg and Rachael.

Adam has formally asked me to marry him and the village is caught up in the preparations. They are anxious to see us settled, not only because they believe so whole-heartedly that love, marriage, families, and happiness go together, but because winter is fast approaching. It will be milder than we are used to on the prairie—our location in such a deep valley is a factor as well as our proximity to a large natural hot springs—but still the villagers need time to concentrate on harvest and preparations for the cold season.

When the village has gathered for meals—with the advent of the colder weather we have moved indoors to tables set up in the cooking house—it pleases me to see our little group from Master's sitting together.

Ross and Mia have had a hard time adjusting to Adam, although he tries very hard to leave his old life behind. Daily, however, I can see changes in them also, and I know that friendship is not far away.

One young man from the village has become a friend to Meg and he often joins us, holding her baby while she eats. His easy laughter and comfortable ways help us all to feel relaxed and better able to enjoy one-another's company.

When we are all together, I often look at Jack. Frail. Stooped. Shrunken.

One could easily misjudge him.

I know the Masters did.

But Jack has a will and spirit that belies his physical shape. And it is those qualities that brought us safely to this wonderful place. That saved all of us.

I will never be able to express my gratitude.

Perhaps as time passes, maybe with the coming of spring, we will be able to truly put the past behind us, forget what we were raised with and live fully as free people.

It will take some care and a lot of effort, for we fall easily into the roles we had, but with enough love and encouragement, we will be able to forget the Before Times forever.

About the Author:

Born on a ranch in Southern Alberta and raised by a family of writers, Diane Stringam Tolley caught the bug early, publishing her first story at the age of 11. Trained in Journalism, she has written countless novels, articles, short stories, plays, songs and poems. Her award-winning novel, Daughter of Ishmael and its sequel, A House Divided are in stores now.

Christmas books, Carving Angels and Kris Kringle's Magic have become perennial family favourites.

Photo Credit:
David Handschuh

Tolley and her Husband live in Northern Alberta and are the parents to six and grandparents to eighteen.

She'd love to hear from you!
dstringamtolley@gmail.com

If you enjoyed
After the Before Times: The Shadows of Innocence,
you might also enjoy these books
by the same author available on Amazon:

Carving Angels
Magic
Gnome for Christmas
SnowMan
Words
Essence
Essence: A Second Dose
Essence: Side Effects
Daughter of Ishmael
Daughters of Ishmael 2: A House Divided
Daughters of Ishmael 3: Deborah
Daughters of Ishmael 4: Abigail
High Water
Ghost of the Overlook
Devon
Melissa
The Babysitter
Blessed by a Curse
Tom, Becoming
God's Tree
The Shining Place
Lili and Peri
Real Estates
Real Estates: The Second Storey
Hosts, Too

Manufactured by Amazon.ca
Acheson, AB

15011629R00125